MW01698606

Chance and Circumstance

A Chance Colt Literary Mystery

Tom Hawks

MAN CAN BE DESTROYED
BUT NOT DEFEATED.

BRIGHTON PUBLISHING LLC
435 N. HARRIS DRIVE
MESA, AZ 85203

Chance and Circumstance

A Chance Colt Literary Mystery

Tom Hawks

Brighton Publishing LLC
435 N. Harris Drive
Mesa, AZ 85203

Brighton Publishing.com

ISBN13: 978-1-62183-394-9

ISBN 10: 1-62183-394-1

Printed in the United States of America

Copyright © 2016

First Edition

Cover Design: Tom Rodriguez

All rights reserved. This is a work of fiction and a creation of the author's imagination. No part of this publication may be reproduced or transmitted in any form or by any means, electronic or mechanical, including photocopy, recording, or any information storage retrieval system, without permission in writing from the copyright owner.

Dedication

This book is dedicated to all of the men and women of American law enforcement; past, present and future. You are truly the "thin blue line" that separates the good guys from the bad guys. May God walk with you, protect you and always remain by your side.

~Tom Hawks

Chapter One

"Santa Cruz to Unit 10," the police radio blurted out, temporarily suspending the peace and quiet of a sun-kissed and warm early spring Sonoran desert afternoon.

"This is Unit 10. Go."

"Unit 10, we have a report of gun shots fired at 323 W. McKeown Avenue in Patagonia."

"10-4. I'm 10-76, en route. Isn't that Charlie Danforth's place?"

"That's affirmative," replied the county dispatcher.

"10-4, Santa Cruz. Unit 10 is in the vicinity. I should be 10-23 in less than five minutes."

Sheriff Chance Colt of Santa Cruz County, Arizona, hung up the mic on his Motorola radio, started his 1989 bright blue metallic Chevy K-5 Blazer with its 350 cubic inch 5.7 liter V-8 engine, and sped to the location as fast as the old 4X4 truck would take him. He flipped on the light bar and siren, blaring all the way into the small mountain town of Patagonia, population 896.

As he approached the address, Sheriff Colt slowed and then stopped his vehicle just short of Charlie Danforth's front yard and turned off the lights and siren. Chance could see the old man sitting in an ancient green-and-white lawn chair, a Smith and Wesson .357 Magnum revolver in his right hand, currently pointed at the bright blue sky. Chance also saw an open Coors beer can sitting in the grass next to Charlie's lawn chair.

"Dispatch, this is Unit 10. I'm 10-23, on the scene." Chance turned off the ignition, unsecured his seatbelt and slowly opened his driver's side door. He stood behind it and the rest of his vehicle for his own safety and cover from the man with the gun. "Afternoon, Charlie!" he called out. "Can you please put the gun down so I can have a chat with you?"

"Howdy, Sheriff. By all means, come on over and have a beer with me. Just watch out for all the darn rattlesnakes sunnin' themselves in the grass here like their havin' a picnic at the beach. This warm weather has brought 'em all outta their holes."

"Charlie, put the gun down on the ground first, away from your chair, and then I'd be glad to join you. I just don't feel like gettin' shot today, if you know what I mean."

With that, Charlie slowly leaned over, almost falling out of his chair, set the gun down in the grass, and held up his two empty hands for the sheriff to see. "Oh, I ain't gonna shoot ya, Sheriff. You're the law. I'm just shootin' snakes."

"Thanks, Charlie." Chance shut the truck door and slowly walked into the yard and up to Charlie with a slight grin on his face, his eyes sharply focused on Charlie's empty hands. "If you don't mind, I'm going to pick up your pistol and unload it for you."

He bent down and picked up the weapon, quickly opened the cylinder with his left thumb on the release, and emptied six live .357 rounds into his right hand. He nonchalantly placed them in the right back pocket of his dark brown uniform pants. Then he set the pistol back down in the grass behind him and reached out to shake Charlie's hand. Chance smiled and looked around a full three hundred and sixty degrees, scanning his surroundings for any other dangers lurking about.

"How you doin,' Charlie?" he asked politely, while smelling the beer on the old man's breath. "Are you alone?"

"Well of course I'm alone, I've been alone for forty years, give or take a few. But these damn rattlesnakes won't leave me be. They come to visit me while I'm tryin' to relax and unwind in my own front yard, just sittin' here bein' all quiet and peaceful as a church mouse, until I hear and see these damn rattlers." Charlie pointed a gnarled index finger at three dead Sonoran sidewinders that lay approximately ten feet in front of his chair. "Can't get no peace with them sons of bitches hangin' round."

"How many shots did it take you to get all three?" Chance asked with genuine interest.

"Three snakes, three shots," Charlie exclaimed. "I may be old, but I still got a steady shootin' hand and eyes like a hawk, I tell you."

"That's some fine shooting," Chance replied, "but you're kinda scarin' the neighbors, the tourists, and the bird watchers."

"Oh, to hell with the bird watchers. I'll shoot them and their damn precious birds too if I get the chance."

"Charlie, you can't go shooting the birds—it's against the law seein' as they're endangered species and all. And I know how you feel about the old snowbirds, but you can't go shooting any tourists either. What would that do for our local economy? We need the tourists and bird watchers to support this county. Where would this county be without the tourists and snowbirds?"

"Where would we be? I'll tell you where we'd be—all alone and enjoyin' some peace and quiet, that's where, damn it, Sheriff!"

"Okay Charlie, settle down and quit your cussin'. I think there's been enough shootin' and killin' around here for one day." Chance pointed at the three dead snakes. "I don't want to have to come back and arrest you for disturbing the peace, or worse. Can we both agree on that?"

"Aw, hell—I guess so, if you insist. You took my last six rounds anyway." Charlie gave him a toothless smile. "I got to go to the gun shop and re-stock, but they're closed on Sundays. So the two-legged tourist snakes and the rattlesnakes are all safe for another day. You caught me empty-handed and out of ammunition."

"That's good news. Now we can all rest easy for the rest of the evening, if you'll promise me you'll be good."

"I promise," Charlie said with a smirk. "Hey, you want a Coors?"

"Thanks anyway, but not while I'm on duty. You take good care of yourself, and I'll be seein' you around."

"Not if I see you first, Sheriff," Charlie said with a laugh. "Remember, I got them hawk eyes."

"Right," Chance smiled politely. "You have a good night, and remember to help me keep the peace around here by behavin' yourself for the rest of the night, okay?"

"I said I was outta ammo, didn't I? Why can't you just leave an old man alone and go out and find some real criminals?"

"I'll do that, Charlie. You have a quiet and peaceful night now, you hear?" Chance tipped the brim of his brown cowboy hat with a two-fingered salute and walked back to his vehicle. He started up the truck, waved once more to Charlie, put the Blazer in gear, and slowly drove up the street of the little town.

He grabbed the mic from his Motorola radio and keyed it up. "Santa Cruz dispatch, this is Unit 10, and I'm 10-8. All is quiet once more on the western front, and I'm back in service."

"10-4, Sheriff. Why don't you call it a day, Chance?"

"I think I'll take you up on that offer, Shirley. I've had enough servin' and protectin' for one day. I'll be headin' home to Sonoita and the little woman. See you in the morning, bright and early."

"Have a good night, Sheriff."

"You too, and tell Don I said hello."

With that, Sheriff Chance Colt started his short drive home to his little ranch in Sonoita and called it a day. He was tired and hungry, and he was looking forward to a hot meal and a nice, quiet, relaxing evening with Sarah.

"Abe Lincoln may have freed all men, but Sam Colt made them equal."

~Famous post-Civil War quote—author unknown

My unwed mother named me Chance because she didn't think I'd have one. My father named me Colt because of natural circumstances. The story goes that my father's last name was Colt, supposedly a true life descendant of the legendary American gun manufacturer, Samuel Colt, the inventor of the Peacemaker—the gun that won the West. It could be a true story or it could be a damn lie. Either way, it doesn't make much difference to me. I am who I am.

My full name is Chance Samuel Colt. I guess one could say chance and circumstance made me into who and what I am today: the elected sheriff of Santa Cruz County, the smallest of fifteen counties in the great state of Arizona. Santa Cruz, which means "Holy Cross" in Spanish, was founded in 1899. Some locals like to joke that it really means "Holy Shit" in Spanish, but those are just the naysayers.

Santa Cruz County covers 1,238 square miles of mountains, rolling hills, and desert. More than 1,230 square miles are land, and only 1.2 square miles are water, making it one of the driest and dustiest places in the country with its rugged, hot, and deadly terrain. It's smack dab in the middle of No Man's Land in the Sonoran Desert and shares a border with Mexico to the south.

The population, as of a recent census, was 46,768 hearty souls. Its demographics are eighty-two percent Hispanic, sixteen percent White, and two percent American Indian, if you believe the census takers. (I know I don't.) The county seat is Nogales, Arizona, which sits right across the international border from its sister city, Nogales, Mexico.

I've had the distinct honor of being the longest-tenured sheriff this God-forsaken county has ever seen, going on twenty-five years. I guess that makes me either too dumb or too stubborn to quit, but law enforcement and keeping the peace are the only things I truly know how to do.

If my ancestry is true and accurate, then my great, great grandfather, Samuel Colt, had a saying that I like—and it still rings true today: "The good people in this world are very far from being satisfied with each other, and my firearms are the best peacemaker." Hence the nickname of his famous pistol.

Speaking of firearms, the state of Arizona has some of the loosest gun laws in the United States. Arizona allows its citizens to carry open or concealed weapons with no permit or license.

In many respects, Arizona is still a lot like the old Wild West, with Santa Cruz County being particularly on the wilder side. One could say that Santa Cruz County was born to be wild and always will be, if the bad guys continue to have their way. It's mostly a rural open-range county that has twice as many old ghost towns as real, inhabitable towns (there are twenty officially registered ghost towns and only ten real towns). Some of the towns can't really, in all fairness, even be called towns. They're legally defined by Arizona and the U.S. government as "Census Designated Places," whatever the hell that means.

The three largest towns are Nogales, population 20,837; Rio Rico, population 18,962; and, coming in at number three in size, Tubac, population 1,191. The other seven towns or "census designated places" are Sonoita, Elgin, Patagonia, Amado, Tumacacori-Carmen, Beyerville, and Kino Springs, all with populations of less than 1,000 inhabitants.

These towns combined are known locally as "The Mountain Empire," although I'm not sure I'd call it an empire of anything except rock, sand, and sky. But this little empire is where I've called home for most of my life. It may not be much, but it's all I've got. And I've sworn to serve and protect it, till death or retirement do us part—whichever comes first.

Towns aside, Santa Cruz is mostly made up of rural, small ranching communities, with a few vineyards and wineries thrown in to spice things up a little. If you like open space, we've got it in spades around here, because the rest of the county consists of mainly wide-open spaces, big skies, rugged mountains, brutal desert, and rolling grasslands. If you are looking for a home where the proverbial buffalo roam, you've come to the right place. Unfortunately, there aren't many buffalo left, but there are plenty of horses, cows, chickens, black bears, mountain lions, bobcats, wolves, coyotes, rattlesnakes, Gila monsters, lizards, scorpions, tarantulas, and black widow and brown recluse spiders for all to experience and enjoy.

And if those aren't enough dangerous animals, reptiles, and Araneae for you, we also have plenty of the two-legged variety of dangerous animals and predators, thanks to the drug runners, drug cartels, and drug mules, as well as the illegal Mexican immigrants crossing the border into our county every day. Together they cause their fair share of fun, excitement, and trouble for law enforcement and the general citizenry along the way.

The great playwright and philosopher William Shakespeare, in his play *As You Like It,* described the seven stages of a man's life, sometimes referred to as "The Seven Stages of Man." They are Infant, School Boy, Lover, Soldier, Justice, Pantaloon, and Old Age. I've lived and survived through several of these stages to date. Sometimes, I think I'm permanently stuck somewhere in the middle of the three middle stages: Lover, Soldier, and Justice. Pantaloon—the quest for money, power, and greed—never much interested a man like me. I'm a simple man with a simple plan, happy and content to live out his life by the Code of the West.

Lately, though, I feel more and more like an old, worn-down, worn-out dinosaur dragging himself slowly but surely to old age and eventual extinction. I just hope God will have some pity on me and let me live long enough to get to experience a small portion of that stage of old age, wisdom, and inner peace that Shakespeare was talking about.

In the meantime, I guess I'll just keep being who I am and doing what I do, like my great, great grandfather tried to do: Keep the peace and be the best lawman I can be. Sometimes, to be honest, I feel like I really don't *want* to do it anymore. I feel more like I *have* to do it—like it's my only true destiny and real purpose in life. I feel like I owe it to ol' Sam Colt and the rest of my ancestors, as well as the decent, hard-working, upstanding citizens who still call this "Wild West" Santa Cruz County home.

If what ol' Bill Shakespeare said is true—"If all the world's a stage, and each of us must play a part"—I guess I was one of the unlucky ones to have been given the part of being born one-hundred years too late; a 19th century lawman living in a 20th and 21st century world. However, a man has to play the cards he was dealt, even if he was dealt the "Dead Man's Hand" of Aces and eights, just like Ole' Wild Bill Hickok.

So by definition, I imagine my name suits me well: Chance Colt. If you look up the word "chance" in the dictionary, you'll find something like:

1. Noun: A possibility of something happening.

2. Noun: The occurrence and development of events in the absence of any obvious design.

3. Adjective: Fortuitous; accidental.

4. Verb: To do something by accident or without design.

5. Verb: To do something
dangerous or of uncertain outcome.

If you look up the word "colt" in the
find:

1. A young male horse, usually belo
four that is not castrated.

2. A young, untried, inexperienced pers

If these definitions don't sum up the young me and the old me, the past me and the present me, and my entire life up to this point in a nutshell, then I don't know what does.

I like to think that time and life experience has wisened me up a bit since the days of my youth. But sometimes, when I look out at this world and this county of Santa Cruz today in the twenty-first century, I have to shake my head in amazement and wonder if I've learned or accomplished anything at all. All I know for sure is I'm not getting any younger and I'm not sure how much longer I can keep riding this old bronco before he bucks me off and stomps me to death, like some old, broken-down rodeo cowboy who can no longer hang on for eight more seconds.

Its hell gettin' old, but I guess it beats pushing up daisies—or cactus, depending on what part of the country you live in. Me, I live in the hot, dry, evil Sonoran Desert. If this place ain't hell itself, then hell's got to be somewhere just around the corner.

Chapter Two

As the sun begins to sink behind the Santa Rita Mountains off to the west, I pull the Blazer into the gravel and sand mile-long driveway and slowly meander my way up to the old homestead. It's a two-story log cabin built on my little hundred-acre ranch appropriately named—to me, at least—"The Sanctuary Ranch." That's exactly what it is for me at this stage in my life.

I spot Sarah over in the round training corral in front of our red and white barn; she's attempting to round up our two horses, Butch and Sundance, so she can brush them down. Then she'll lead them into their stalls in the barn to feed them their dinner.

My heart jumps a little at the sight of Sarah, looking fit and trim in her tight Wrangler jeans, blue denim shirt with the sleeves rolled up to her elbows, and dusty, well-worn cowboy boots. She's forty-five years old, but with her curvy, athletic figure she could easily pass for thirty-five. It must be the fresh, clean country air that keeps her looking so good. Her long blonde hair hangs down to the middle of her back in a neat braid; a ball cap keeps the dust off. She is silhouetted in the setting sun, and I can clearly see the outline of her large, firm breasts under her shirt, making for quite a pretty picture after a long, hard day of work.

As I pull the Blazer up near the house and park, Sarah greets me with a wave of her hand and a warm smile. I pull my stiff, aching body from the truck, shut the door, and gaze at my youthful-looking wife, wondering to myself why she still looks so young and vibrant while I feel as old and tired as the hills and mountains I can see in all directions around our little ranch. I smile and wave back and start slowly walking toward the round corral.

I am also enthusiastically welcomed home by my other best friend and trusty life companion, William Shakespeare, my carefree and forever fun-loving black Labrador retriever. He greets me like he hasn't seen me in ten years; in reality it's only been ten hours since I left him at the front door this morning as I was heading off to work. Who knows how long it feels in "dog time" to him?

"How you doin', Shake and Bake?" I call out to him. He jumps on me and I vigorously pet him, returning the welcome of my loyal friend and sidekick. *God I love dogs*, I think to myself. *Dogs and horses are some of the finest people I've ever known.*

"Howdy, Sheriff!" Sarah has closed the corral gate behind her and walked up next to us, slapping the dust off her thighs. She gives me a warm kiss and a smile. "Glad to have you home. A woman can get mighty lonely in these parts, you know," she says with a laugh.

"Hey, Sarah." I'm a man of few words, the strong and silent type, so I give her a bear hug. Even after all these years, the feel of her firm breasts against my chest gives me an instant erection and a slight tingle in the family jewels.

"It looks like somebody else is happy to see me too," she says as she looks down at the bulge in my pants.

"Hey, I may be gettin' old, but I ain't dead yet. I'll help you finish brushing down the horses and putting them away for the night, and, then maybe we can enjoy a little roll in the hay ourselves before dinner."

"Somebody's feeling a little frisky today, huh? You look tired and worn out. Are you sure you have the energy?"

"No, and I might die in the middle of it, but there's worse ways to go," I say with a laugh. "I'm willing to take the chance if you are."

"Works for me. A woman needs to get it where and when she can nowadays." She slaps my butt and laughs before sauntering away from me and back to the horses.

Sarah and Chance brushed down Butch and Sundance, put them up in their stalls, and gave them food and water for the night. Then they climbed up to the cozy hayloft and had a little fun on a couple of horse blankets, like two high school kids sneaking away to have sex in her daddy's barn.

Afterward, they dressed and walked hand-in-hand through the darkening dusk of the early evening to the main house, with William Shakespeare leading the way. After a quiet dinner of green salad, fried chicken, mashed potatoes, and biscuits with country gravy, they sat in their rocking chairs in the living room and commenced with intimate conversation about each other's day. A fire burned low in the flagstone fireplace, lending comforting heat in the cool of the evening.

As Chance listened to his wife talk, he leaned back, taking in the stained pine log walls and fifteen-foot-high wood-beam ceiling before closing his eyes and letting the weight of the world slip off his shoulders. Shakespeare lay on the floor between their chairs, chewing on his rawhide bone with a look of quiet contentment and peaceful bliss radiating from his dark brown eyes. All was well with the world.

Three decades earlier, Sarah and Chance had first met at the University of Arizona, when Tucson was still a quiet, peaceful, slow-paced cowboy town. Sarah had earned her bachelor's degree in archeology while Chance had majored in criminal justice sciences with a minor in philosophy. Chance had imagined himself, back then, as a cross between Wyatt Earp and Socrates: a thinking man's lawman. The "dichotomy of man" was how he used to like to explain it to people who inquired. In his words and in his mind, he intended to become a peaceful warrior of the Wild West—a sort of Clint Eastwood/Zen Master.

A lot had changed since back then. In fact, the whole world had changed. Tucson no longer was just a quiet little cowboy town; it had become a big-city oasis and a haven for drug dealers, crack addicts, and gang-bangers. Santa Cruz County had turned into a hotspot for illegal immigrant border crossings and was the main route of illegal drugs and narcotics coming out of Mexico and being trafficked and sold in Arizona and shipped off to all points across the United States by organized crime syndicates and the drug cartels, drug runners, and drug mules of Mexico.

Somehow, some way, Sarah and Chance were still the same two people they always were. Sarah still got her kicks by digging up rocks, fossils, and old bones, and Chance still tried his best to balance his dueling inner Zen Buddhist philosophies with his sworn oath to uphold the law of the land, the Code of the West, and to fight the never-ending battle between good and evil.

After a lull in the conversation, during which Chance had almost fallen asleep, he roused himself and picked up one of his favorite books. Soon he was absorbed in *Zen and the Art of Motorcycle Maintenance* by Robert M. Pirsig, which he was reading for probably the fiftieth time, while Sarah was reading the latest copy of *Arizona Highways*. Shakespeare was gnawing on his bone and, probably, silently quoting himself.

At about 2200 hours, Chance kissed Sarah goodnight, bade Mr. Shakespeare a pleasant evening, and headed upstairs to hit the sack for the night. He had an early morning meeting down at the Nogales Sheriff's Station, and he was worn out from the day's activities and needed some shut-eye. He was sound asleep ten minutes after his head hit the pillow.

On April 26, 1921, a small group of Mexican *banditos* raided the Ruby Mercantile in Ruby, Arizona. The owners, Frank Pearson and his wife, Myrtle, were killed by two of the bandits during the robbery. A man named George J. White was the sheriff of Santa Cruz County at the time. It took Sheriff White a year to solve the crime; eventually two Mexican men named Placidio Silvas and Manuel Martinez were arrested, tried, and convicted of the murders. Silvas was sentenced to life in prison; Martinez received the death sentence—execution by hanging.

On the evening of July 13, 1922, Sheriff White and his deputy Leonard A. Smith left Nogales to transport the two prisoners by automobile to the state prison in Florence, Arizona. As luck would have it, the vehicle crashed and overturned in a dry wash on the Nogales Highway, in the area that is now the town of Sahuarita. The prisoners broke free and bludgeoned the sheriff and deputy; Sheriff White was later found dead at the scene, while Deputy Smith was severely injured and died later.

Both Mexican prisoners escaped unharmed into the empty desert. More than seven hundred volunteers from surrounding counties formed posses and searched the area in and around the accident site for nearly a week. Both prisoners were eventually recaptured and taken up to the state prison in Florence by the newly sworn in Santa Cruz County sheriff, Harry Saxon, and his deputies.

Manuel Martinez was re-tried, re-sentenced, and eventually hanged for his crimes; Placidio Silvas was again given a life sentence, but he escaped prison in 1928 and was never seen again.

Sheriff George White was survived by a wife, two daughters, and one son.

At close to midnight, I awoke in a cold sweat after dreaming of the death of the Sheriff George White on that fateful drive up to the state prison in Florence in 1921. It wasn't the first time I had had this dream. This may seem kind of strange or silly to most people, but ever since the day I was sworn in as sheriff of Santa Cruz County I've often had recurring nightmares and dreams about the deceased lawman. Call me crazy, but sometimes I can even feel his other-worldly presence sitting next to me in my truck or standing or walking with me as I perform my daily duties as sheriff. It's almost as if the murdered sheriff has become my silent, invisible partner and guardian angel on the job with me for all my years as sheriff. I know it sounds strange, but it feels true enough to me.

You might think I'm an overly superstitious cop with an overactive imagination, but in all my years of law enforcement, I've come to believe in signs, both from this world and from the great beyond. And I know from life experience that I can always use the extra help, even if it's from a dead guy's ghost.

As I awoke from my recurring dream on this particular night, I got out of bed and looked out my window. In the darkness I saw the old, familiar great horned owl resting comfortably on a limb of the tree closest to my bedroom window, his head turned toward me and his narrow yellow eyes glaring at me. Lately he had become an increasingly frequent visitor of mine. As always, I felt my blood turn to ice in my veins. It seemed the messenger from the dead (as the Native American culture believes owls to be) and my guardian angel, Sheriff White, had come to give me a warning or a sign that something bad was about to happen in my neck of the woods—or, more accurately, in my neck of the evil Sonoran Desert.

I went to the bathroom, splashed some cold water on my face, and attempted to go back to sleep, but I mostly just tossed and turned, my mind racing, for the next two hours. Until my cell phone rang.

I spotted it in the dark and grabbed it, answering before it could ring a third time and wake Sarah. "Sheriff Colt," I said into the phone as I stepped out into the hall, closing the bedroom door behind me.

"I'm sorry to bother you, Sheriff, but we just found a cold one," Deputy Graves sputtered.

"No problem, Deputy. I've been expecting your call," I stated.

"You expected my call?" Graves sounded surprised.

"Yeah, don't ask me why. I just had a feeling. What have you got?"

"Well, it's an odd one all right, but what we got is a naked and dead Indian hung up in a tree just off I-19 in Tubac on Kenyon Ranch Road. He's about a mile west of I-19 hanging from a big ol' mesquite tree about twenty feet off the edge of the road."

"Hanging by what?" growled Chance.

"Hangin' by a rope with a noose tied around his neck."

"I'll be there in twenty-five minutes, so don't leave or touch the scene. Just secure it till I get there."

"Yes, sir. Me and the dead Indian will just be hangin' around, so to speak, waitin' on you," Graves chuckled. "One more unusual thing you should know about this one, though."

"What's that?"

"Well, sir, his private parts are sort of cut off and are stuffed in his mouth."

"Say again?"

"His penis and testicles look like they were cut off with a knife, and somebody shoved them up inside his mouth."

"Got it. Don't touch anything. I'll see you there."

Chance hung up the cell phone and dressed quickly in his jeans, flannel shirt, and uniform jacket. He gave Sarah a quick peck on the cheek; she stirred, mumbled "Bye," and turned over and went back to sleep. She was used to this. He clipped his off-duty weapon, a 1911 Colt .45, into its holster and onto his belt, pulled on his brown cowboy boots and hat, grabbed the truck keys, and raced down the stairs and out of the house to his truck.

On his way to the scene, Chance used his cell phone to call Alexis Montoya, his best and most seasoned detective. She also happened to be his favorite. She answered on the third ring.

"Montoya," she said in a half-whisper.

"Alexis, this is Chance. I'm sorry to wake you, but I need your help. We've got a dead body hanging from a mesquite tree in Tubac, and I want you to be lead on the investigation."

"You got it," she answered. "What's the location?"

He gave Detective Montoya the directions just as he arrived on scene himself. In his headlights, he could see Deputy Graves leaning on the hood of his squad car eating his lunch, which he had spread across the hood of his police vehicle like he was having a Sunday picnic in the park. Graves waved to the sheriff as he pulled up in the Blazer.

Chance could also see in his headlights the twisted, naked, blue-grey and bloody body of the dead man hanging from a thick branch of the mesquite tree. A rope noose was tied around his neck; the other end of the rope was tied tightly to the tree. A pool of blood had darkened a circle of sand on the bare ground underneath him.

The sound of Montoya's voice in his ear drew him back to the phone call. "I'll be there in fifteen minutes," she said. "I live in Tubac."

"Take your time, Alexis," he said. "I don't think the victim is going anywhere soon."

"You say victim?" Montoya asked. "Do you think it's a suicide or a murder?"

"Well, I'm no Medical Examiner, but I think I can go out on a limb here—no pun intended—and say it isn't a suicide."

"Why's that?" asked Montoya.

"Because right now, the victim has his mouth full of his own bloody penis and testicles. Looks to me like he was castrated like a Brahma bull by a butcher. That's why. Of course, again, I'm no M.E., I'm just an old, dumb county sheriff, but that would be my initial guess. I just arrived at the scene, so I'll have to take a closer look to be sure, but I'd be willing to bet my own family jewels this ain't no suicide. What we have here is a bold and clear statement someone is tryin' to make."

"Jesus Christ, Chance! I'll be there in five. What the hell is this world coming to? This used to be such a nice, quiet county."

"Oh, believe me, it's still nice and quiet. All I can hear out here is the sweet sound of Deputy Graves chewing on his ham and cheese sandwich, and the soft swaying of a dead Indian hanging from a tree in the light breeze coming in from the southwest on a cloudless southern Arizona night."

"Wow. You make a murder scene sound almost poetic, Chance."

"Murder is poetry in its coldest and darkest form. It's all in the way that you look at things, Alexis. See you soon." Chance hung up the phone and smiled sarcastically at Deputy Graves. "Enjoying your picnic?"

Chapter Three

Sheriff Chance Colt had seen a lot of death in his life and in his time, first as a U.S. Marine in the Persian Gulf War, and later in the battle of Mogadishu in East Africa and a few other similar top secret missions and skirmishes in the early stages of the Afghanistan and Iraq conflicts. And then, unfortunately, he had experienced more death as an Arizona lawman.

In every death he had ever witnessed, it always appeared in a strange sense to him to be ironically peaceful. Even today, in this Indian's death, there was a feeling of peace at the scene that hung heavy in the air but was hard to define. *Maybe this feeling is what heaven is like,* he thought to himself, *and everyone's worldly life is hell.*

It seemed to Chance that the most precious gift God had given each person was the gift of time: time to spend in quiet contemplation within yourself, time to spend with your family, time to spend with friends, time to work and time to play; time to laugh, and time to cry; time to live, and time to die. So, Chance thought, the lesson was to spend your time wisely and not frivolously. Don't waste it away, for it is a gift from God that is timeless in and of itself. And once you run out of time, it's gone forever. Gone forever, and lost in the deep, dark abyss of complete and utter emptiness.

Why does a dead body always look so peaceful, he wondered, *even the body of this man who was so obviously brutally murdered? Maybe it was because the ordeal or the suffering of life was finally over. He lived a life of hell, and his reward for that was now heaven and eternal peace. At his death, one finally gets to experience the peace he has always searched for in his life. Maybe that's it? Maybe one has to experience hell before he's presented with the gift of heaven and the feeling of true and final peace.*

Only God and the dead knew the answer, but Chance liked to believe it was true. That belief was what got him through each day, until his own time of death came.

Chance was pulled out of his deep thoughts at the sound of Montoya's Dodge Charger pulling up to the scene, with its Hemi engine and characteristic low, guttural growl of the dual exhaust. He turned toward the noise and was almost unnerved by the sight of Deputy Graves staring directly into his face, his mouth slightly agape and a dab of mustard on his dimpled chin.

"Are you all right, Sheriff?" asked Graves. "It seemed like I lost you there for a minute."

"I was just thinking through the crime scene. Do me a favor and radio into dispatch for the evidence tech to get out here to work up the scene."

"Roger that, Chief," Graves said.

Chance rolled his eyes; he couldn't help it. "How many times have I told you not to call me chief? Do I look like a damn Indian chief to you?"

"No sir, you sure don't."

"Then quit calling me chief and call me sheriff. Now get on your radio and get that E.T. out here pronto."

Detective Montoya had exited her vehicle and walked up to Chance and the crime scene. He turned his attention to her and smiled. "Nice night for a hangin', don't you think? It's good to see you. How've you been?"

"Oh, I've been hanging in there," she said with a wide, Colgate-white smile. "Looks like I'm not the only one hanging though."

"You look beautiful as always," said Chance, "even when you get called out of bed at three o'clock in the morning."

"And you look like shit, Sheriff. Don't you ever get any sleep?"

"I try, but this darn sheriff job keeps gettin' in the way. I guess I can sleep when I'm dead."

"Nice truck, Sheriff." Alexis pointed at Chance's '89 Blazer. "When are you finally going to give up that old dinosaur and get yourself a new vehicle?"

"That Blazer is a K-5 classic." He smiled as he admired his old truck. "She runs like a top and still has a lot of life left in her. They don't make 'em like that anymore. She's still a beast."

"A dinosaur beast," Alexis laughed. "It's practically an antique, for god's sake."

"I like old trucks. They have character and charisma that the new ones just don't have. Besides, old is the new new, haven't you heard? Old trucks are like old men and old wine: they just keep getting better and better with time."

"I think you should take her out back of the Sheriff's Station and shoot her to put her out of her misery. Can she even go fifty-five at this point?"

"On a good day, she can still do sixty-five if she has to. I've got no need to go much faster than that. The world's round, right? So I'll get there eventually. People are in such a hurry nowadays. Nobody takes the time anymore to stop and smell the roses along the way—or the dead corpses, for that matter."

"Speaking of corpses, Sheriff, what do we have here tonight?" Alexis asked.

"What we've got here is a dead Indian and a murder investigation."

"What gave you your first clue, Sherlock?" She smiled sarcastically.

"Why, the deceased human body over there, of course." Chance pointed toward the tree. "Shall we take a look-see before the E.T. shows up and destroys the crime scene?"

"Why, of course. After you."

"Ladies first, ma'am. I insist." Chance gave a courtly wave, gesturing for the detective to go first.

"Why thank you, Sheriff—you're always such a gentleman. But if you don't mind, I'd like to put some rubber gloves on first."

"Why, of course. We wouldn't want you comin' into contact with any pesky blood-borne pathogens, now would we?"

Deputy Graves stood there dumbfounded, looking at both the detective and the sheriff as if they were both certifiably nuts.

"Did you call out the E.T., Graves?" the sheriff growled sternly.

"Yes sir, Sheriff."

"Well, then, you can give your written statement to Detective Montoya, since she'll be the lead detective on this one. Then you can shove off and be on your merry way to your next call."

"Thank you, Sheriff. Enjoy your night," said Graves.

"Oh, it's always a pleasure to work with you, Graves, and I'll have a great night. Nothin' beats the smell of a dead, rotting corpse in the desert heat as the sun is coming up. You take care now, deputy, and be safe out there. Hopefully you won't find any more dead bodies tonight."

"It don't matter to me, Sheriff. I get paid by the hour." Deputy Graves went back to his vehicle to write his report as the first responder to the scene for Detective Montoya's investigation.

After Deputy Graves went 10-8 and back into service, Detective Montoya and Sheriff Colt parked their respective vehicles with their headlights directed onto the murder scene. The E.T. would need as much light as possible on the dead body in the early morning desert dawn of a new day in Santa Cruz County. They diligently went to work on the crime scene investigation before the temperature started getting too hot and the corpse too ripe.

Detective Alexis Montoya was what Sheriff Colt would describe as "a real looker." She was in her mid-thirties, with beautiful classic Hispanic features: flawless almond-colored skin, high cheekbones, full pouty lips, smoldering dark brown eyes and long, silky, shiny straight black hair hanging down to her slim waistline when it wasn't tied back for work. She was approximately five-feet-four inches tall, about one hundred and ten pounds, with small but round and perky breasts, tan and shapely legs, and a butt you couldn't help but follow with your eyes as she sashayed down the street. But it was those fiery, sexy, smoldering, dark brown bedroom eyes that could mesmerize a man. Chance thought to himself that one could easily spend a lifetime gazing into those beautiful eyes and completely forget that anything else in the world existed. Detective Montoya was the one female cop in the sheriff's department that nearly every male pursued, hunted, or at least lusted after with vigor.

Alexis had a fiery personality that very much rivaled and matched her sultry and fiery eyes. She was not-so-affectionately known around the department as "the Ice Princess Bitch with hell's fire in her eyes." Secretly, Chance thought she knew about and liked that moniker.

Alexis had grown up in Nogales, Arizona, in a large but poor Hispanic family. She had married at the young age of nineteen and was verbally, physically, and mentally abused by her scumbag, alcoholic husband—whom she eventually shot and killed one night in self-defense, after taking what she had decided was her last and final beating.

She had emerged from this early-life traumatic experience as a mentally and physically tough, determined, and strong woman with a heart of stone and a streetwise personality that would never fully trust another man again. Alexis was a woman who turned her young, school-girl innocence and weakness into a cold, hardened, determined strength. She was going to save the world and every woman in it from having to endure the same abuse and torture that she had endured at such a young age. She was a tiny but strong-willed firecracker of a woman with an explosive temper and a mean spirit. She seemed to thrive on administering revenge.

Chance had worked and investigated her case at the time she had killed her husband, and he had taken her under his protective wing and helped her rebuild her life and her fragile ego. Because of this relationship and bond between the two of them, they both had learned to trust, love, and respect each other, like two war-weary soldiers who had been through hell and back together. She would take a bullet for him and he for her, without hesitation. Chance had provided Alexis with a second chance at life, and he was the only man in the world she would trust again.

The rest of the male gender received her cold-blooded stares and her hot-tempered personality. Thus, the nickname "Ice Princess" was hard-earned and hard-assed, and her reputation was widely known across the state as a woman who wouldn't take any shit from another human being. Alexis Montoya only let down her guard and trusted two loyal and proven friends: Chance and the four-legged beast, William Shakespeare. Everyone else in this world better stay clear of her and out of her path, or they would experience the intense heat and destruction of this human ball of hell-fire. Chance loved to unleash her fury on the outside world to the unbelieving and unsuspecting male population, and watch her kick some serious ass. She was Santa Cruz County's own version of "Dirty Harriet," and a "Magnum Force" of one.

Chance and Alexis meticulously secured the crime scene and began to scour it for evidence. The dead body wasn't just missing his family jewels; the ring finger of his left hand was also absent and glaringly missing from the scene, as if taken by the killer as a souvenir or trophy to commemorate the occasion and remember his kill.

The E.T. arrived and began taking photos of the victim and murder scene. He methodically collected any and all physical evidence that might prove helpful in solving the case. Besides the deceased body and the rope itself, there were blood specimens to be taken, finger prints and hair samples to be collected, and tire tracks and footprints to be photographed, measured, and imprinted in plaster. A thorough search must be completed in a step-by-step circular radius around the crime scene, starting at the victim's body and slowly working outward a few hundred yards in all directions.

Sheriff Colt recognized a tattoo on the deceased's right bicep depicting a wolf howling at a full moon. Chance had seen this exact tattoo a few times before on other men. It was a tattoo that identified the dead man as a member of an elite group of highly trained and skilled members of a specialized federal law enforcement organization known as the Shadow Wolves.

Chance knew the Shadow Wolves to be a specialized unit made up of Native Americans from several different tribes across the nation, including the Tohono O'odham, Navajo, Lakota Sioux, Blackfeet, Omaha, and Yaqui. They were a unit within the U.S. Immigration and Customs Enforcement (ICE) Agency, based on the Native American Tohono O'odham Nation in southern Arizona. Shadow Wolf agents were specifically known for their ability to track drug smugglers and illegal immigrants as they attempted to smuggle illegal drugs and narcotics across the border from Mexico into the United States.

The unit had an esteemed and proud reputation and history of tracking human beings that had been passed down from generation to generation. The name Shadow Wolves defined the way the unit hunted: like a pack of wolves. When one wolf finds prey, it calls in the rest of the wolf pack.

Despite their training with, possession of, and use of high-tech equipment, they proudly relied mainly on traditional methods of hunting and tracking, primarily a technique called "cutting for sign." Cutting was searching for and analyzing signs, which included any kind of physical evidence such as footprints, tire tracks, thread, clothing, bodily fluids, solids, and the like.

The Shadow Wolf agent's old-fashioned, methodical approach enabled them to track and apprehend smugglers across arduous desert and mountain terrain covering the seventy-six-mile border shared by the Tohono O'odham Nation and Mexico, along with nearly three million acres of Indian reservation land to the north.

An experienced Shadow Wolf had the training and ability to spot small, tiny items of clothing or thread snagged on tree branches, bent or broken twigs and blades of grass, or footprints in the desert sand that might be days old. An agent could even recognize a single fiber of cloth or burlap sack that could have been filled with illegal drugs. The small unit of only fifteen to twenty members had seized thousands of pounds of marijuana, heroin, cocaine, and other illegal drugs and dozens of vehicles. They had arrested hundreds of drug smugglers and human traffickers of illegal immigrants in the years since the unit's inception in 1972.

As soon as Chance noticed the tattoo, he called his friend John Black Chief to come and assist in identifying the deceased. Black Chief was a former classmate of Chance's at the University of Arizona, had majored in criminal justice sciences as well, and was now the agent-in-charge of the Shadow Wolf unit and an employee of the U.S. Immigration and Customs Enforcement agency. Black Chief was also a tribal member of the Tohono O'odham Nation.

Black Chief arrived at the murder scene approximately thirty minutes after Chance had spoken briefly with him on the phone. He drove up in a red GMC Sierra four-wheel drive extended cab pickup truck.

"Nice truck, John," Chance said. "Is it new?"

"A lot newer than your piece of shit Chevy Blazer, old friend," Black Chief responded with a hearty smile and laugh.

"Good to see you." The two men shook hands warmly. "Sorry to call you out so early in the morning, but I think our deceased is one of yours. John, you already know Alexis, and this is Mike Munoz, our evidence tech. Our M.E., Dr. Patel—otherwise known as Dr. Death—will be out here shortly to deliver the body to the lab and help us determine the official cause of death, although it appears pretty apparent."

Agent Black Chief walked closer to the dead body without getting close enough to contaminate the scene. He shook his head, sighed heavily, and announced, "That's Billy Big Bear. And, yes, he is one of ours: a Shadow Wolf."

"I'm sorry, friend," Chance said. "It's hard to lose one of your own. Any idea why would Billy be so far off the reservation? Was he tracking or working a case all the way out here in Tubac?"

"I don't know for sure," Black Chief said, "but I'm sure as hell going to find out."

"We'll do all we can to help," Chance said. "As you can see, the deceased appears to have been hung in style and castrated with a knife, with his genitals placed in his mouth and his left ring finger also cut off. Somebody was tryin' to make a definite statement or leave a strong message by the way this was done."

Alexis stepped up with an evidence bag and showed it to Black Chief. "We also found this bloody eagle feather lying in the pool of blood underneath the body."

Black Chief glanced at the bag and its contents, rubbing his forehead with his hand and sighing again.

"Do you think it was a Mexican drug cartel hit," Chance said, "because Billy was gettin' too close to the assailant with his investigation or tracking? Or do you think it was some kind of enemy act of revenge?"

"It could be a Mexican drug cartel hit, if Billy was getting too close," Black Chief stated. "The Mexicans are known for making a statement by cutting off a man's genitals and putting them in his mouth as a clear act of retribution and a sign to show they're shutting up the victim permanently. But this eagle feather is bothersome to me. This is a sign that the murder may have been committed by another Indian. An eagle feather is sacred to all Indian tribes, and it would have been left here on purpose, as a sign or message of warning or revenge. In the Indian wars of the 1800s, the Apaches often castrated and mutilated the bodies of their enemies as a symbol of revenge."

"The closest Apaches to here would be the White Mountain Apache Tribe on the Fort Apache Indian Reservation. But that's three hours north of here," Chance said. "Why would an Apache want to kill an O'odham?"

"Who knows?" Black Chief shrugged. "Maybe to start up the Indian wars again."

"But why would they start up a war now, over a hundred years later?" asked Chance.

"There's no statute of limitations on revenge. The feeling of revenge burns deep in every man's soul forever," Black Chief stated. "The heat and fire of revenge is a strong emotion that can never be snuffed out completely. It goes on forever for an Indian, passed down from generation to generation."

The four law professionals stood in silent contemplation a long while after this last statement was spoken. The words left a slight, cold chill hanging in the early morning high desert air.

Chapter Four

Twenty-four hours after the hanging victim's estimated time of death, Chance's phone rang. The medical examiner, Dr. Patel, was calling with his findings, based on the test results he had in his possession.

"The victim, Billy Big Bear, had a drug called Rohypnol in his system. Rohypnol is a tranquilizer commonly used in date rape cases, and it usually comes in a pill form that's tasteless and odorless and can be quickly dissolved into any drink. The drug is usually called by its street name, roofies. The effect of a roofie is sedation, which occurs within twenty to thirty minutes after ingestion and can last up to twelve hours."

"I'm pretty sure that ain't what killed him. Am I right?"

"I don't believe Rohypnol was the cause of Billy Big Bear's death," Dr. Patel said. "One dose of Rohypnol probably would have put him to sleep or at least made him semi-conscious, but it wasn't what killed him, in my opinion. I believe the victim died of asphyxiation and a broken neck as the result of being hanged. I also believe that his penis, testicles, and finger were cut off by the assailant postmortem and not before."

"Thanks, Doc." Chance leaned back in his office chair and propped his booted feet comfortably on his vintage oak desk. "If you could send me and Detective Montoya your entire report as soon as possible, it'd be much appreciated. Have a nice day."

Chance hung up the phone, considering this new information as he turned slightly to gaze out the window. His office was on the third floor of the Sheriff's Office Building at 2170 N. Congress Drive, an edifice built like a fortress high on a hill overlooking run-down shacks on both sides of the ugly black steel border wall that separated Nogales, Arizona, from Nogales, Mexico.

"Apache Indian war or Mexican drug cartel assassination?" he said aloud to himself. "I'm gettin' too old for this shit."

He phoned Black Chief and then Alexis and relayed the M.E.'s autopsy report results to them. After that, he thought lunch at the corner diner sounded good, and a subsequent stop out at the crime scene one more time to look for signs would almost finish out his afternoon.

Chance knew the feds would be swooping in soon to take over the investigation before a country bumpkin sheriff accidently botched it up. The feds would arrogantly and impolitely tell him and his department to step aside and let the professionals solve their own case, and he could go back to chasing rattlesnakes, javelinas, or the common livestock of rural Santa Cruz County once again. He sighed, put his feet back on the floor, stretched, and headed for his vehicle.

After a lunch of chicken Caesar salad at Rosalita's Café in Nogales, Chance drove out to the murder scene in Tubac one more time before the feds showed up and stomped all over any currently undiscovered evidence. He stood there silently in the heat of the afternoon sun and studied the scene with all of his senses: sight, sound, smell, taste, and touch. Eventually his sixth sense kicked in, and his old silent partner spoke up.

Looks like an Apache killin' to me, said the familiar voice of the long-dead sheriff, George J. White.

"Why would an Apache come all the way down here from the White Mountains to murder and mutilate Billy Big Bear, a Shadow Wolf," said Chance out loud to the empty earth and sky, "and then intentionally leave an eagle feather as evidence, which would point straight back to an Indian suspect? It just doesn't make sense, George."

You think it was more likely a Mexican drug runner? asked the inner voice.

"Yes I do, George. I think Billy Big Bear was lured off the reservation following his prey and was subsequently discovered and murdered for getting himself too close to his target. All we got for physical evidence is what looks to me like tire prints from a 4X4 pickup and footprints or boot prints, some big like a man's and some small like a woman's or a teenager." Chance walked closer to the tree and gazed up at the branch where the body had been swinging. "But there's no way Billy was stripped naked and murdered in such a sadistic way by a kid. We got blood samples, but all of them match

Billy's blood type. And there ain't no finger prints on the body, so the murderer must've worn gloves."

What else do ya think? White asked him.

"Well, I think Billy knew his assailant, felt comfortable with him, had a drink with him at some bar around here, and that's when he was drugged and driven out here in a pickup truck, unconscious. The assailant used the bed of the pickup to prop him up, then tied the noose around his neck, secured the rope to the mesquite tree, and drove the truck out from underneath him. The weight of Billy's own body broke his neck and cut off his ability to breathe, causing his instant death by hanging."

What about them missing bits?

"The assailant then backed up the truck again under the hanging corpse, cut off the victim's genitals with a hunting knife, and put them in his mouth. Then the assailant drove off into the desert."

Sounds like a sadistic son of a bitch with some strong emotions of revenge, said White. *But why cut off the ring finger too?*

"Because murder is more often than not a crime of passion," replied Chance, "and this kind of passion only comes from two emotions, the two strongest emotions that a human being is capable of: love or hate."

I think ya got somethin' here, son.

"Yes, that's it!" Chance yelled out loud. "This murder was either committed by a drug runner out of his passion of hatred for the Shadow Wolves and ensuring his own survival or it was committed out of the strongest human passion of all: love. That's why the left ring finger was cut off and taken as a trophy. The murderer was a female and cut off Billy's wedding ring in a fit of womanly jealousy and rage," Chance announced triumphantly. "Elementary, my dear Sheriff White—you're brilliant!"

Aw shucks, Sheriff Colt, it was nothin'. It was you who thought of it. I was just tryin' to be of service and lend a hand, or in this case a finger, to another fellow sheriff, White said. *That's why I hang around and assist you. We county sheriffs are our own breed and we've got to stick together.*

Chance jumped up and ran to his old Blazer to call Alexis and Black Chief. He conferenced them in on the call so he didn't have to say everything twice. After he explained his theory and motive for the murder to both of them in detail, the agent and the detective agreed it was one logical explanation for the bizarre murder and mutilation.

Chance asked Alexis to start canvassing the local town bars to see if Billy Big Bear had been a recent visitor to one of the establishments, and to find out who he was accompanied by. Then he requested that Black Chief dig up any dirt on Billy Big Bear's wife and marriage and look into the possibility of Billy having a girlfriend on the side.

He ended the call and turned the key in the ignition to start the Blazer; he was more than eager to race off to follow his new leads. But instead of the old engine roaring to life, all he heard was the click... click... click of a dead electric starter.

"Shit," Chance yelled as he banged his left hand on the truck's steering wheel. Then he sat there quietly for a few minutes, trying to take in and let out a few Zen-like breaths to calm himself down. Once he was of a quieter heart and mind, he radioed dispatch.

"Unit 10 to Santa Cruz County."

"Go ahead, Unit 10."

"Shirley, can you please do me a favor and call Matt's Towing and have a 10-51 sent to my location?"

He gave Shirley his location and settled in for a long, quiet wait. *I'll just sit here peacefully and watch another southern Arizona sunset over the Santa Rita Mountains*, he thought. *And if I get too bored or lonely while I'm waitin', I'll just shoot myself in the foot.*

By the time the tow truck arrived, it was late afternoon and Chance had settled into a peaceful frame of mind once again. He had calmed himself by watching and listening to the sights and sounds of the surrounding desert and mountains and contemplating the murder investigation scene and his latest theory.

Indian war, illegal drug war, or a jilted lover's revenge? he repeatedly questioned himself. Upon seeing the plume of dust that signaled the arrival of the tow truck, he heaved a sigh of relief. *Finally!*

When the truck pulled up, Chance saw that Matt himself had driven the tow truck instead of sending one of his employees. Chance had got acquainted with Matt on a personal basis since Matt was always towing and repairing Chance's old Chevy that he stubbornly refused to give up on. Chance could see the friendly, familiar smile on Matt's face as he exited his tow truck and walked up to the broken-down Blazer.

"Afternoon, Sheriff. What's wrong with her now?" Matt said.

"I think she just doesn't like me anymore. That and I think the starter went bad. All I get when I turn the ignition key is a click, click, click. But that's okay, because waitin' on you has given me plenty of quality alone time to think on some things."

"You've been thinkin'?" Matt said with a laugh. "Thinkin' about what—the meaning of life?"

"That and the art of motorcycle maintenance," replied Chance, with a calm, cool smile on his face.

"The art of what?" said Matt, looking somewhat perplexed.

"Oh, it's not really important, Matt. I was just thinkin'."

"Can you turn her over a couple of times, Sheriff?"

Chance cranked the ignition so Matt could listen to it. After hearing the steady clicking sound, Matt agreed with Chance that it was most likely the electric starter gone bad.

"I'll hook you up and take her in to my shop and drop you off at your station," Matt said. "If it's just the starter I need to replace, I can have her ready for you by tomorrow afternoon."

"Sounds good. As always, I appreciate the help."

Matt grinned as he began hooking the Blazer up to his tow truck. "I know it's none of my business, but when are you goin' to leave the eighties behind and put this old girl out to pasture?"

"When hell freezes over, like I've told you pretty much every time you've asked me that question. I love this truck! We've been through too much history together to give up on her. She's saved my life more'n once."

"I'm afraid one day she's just gonna give up on you. Then you'll be forced to enter the twenty-first century of modern technology and the modern automobile."

"Well, I guess I'll cross that bridge when I get there, amigo. In the meantime, I have you, my trusty mechanic, to keep me drivin' down the road. And, speaking of the eighties, they would be a fine decade to be stuck in, if I recall them correctly. The world was a whole lot simpler and safer back then. Nowadays, this world has gone plum crazy and taken us all along with her, whether we want to go for the ride or not. The world was a lot more peaceful and things made a lot more sense back in those days."

"Yep! I have to agree with you there. The world's gone to hell in a handbasket, as they say. Go ahead and hop in my truck, and I'll finish gettin' this old girl hooked up and get you back to your office."

"Thanks, Matt. I appreciate the rescue, and I owe you a beer sometime." Chance slapped Matt on the back and ambled over to the passenger door of the tow truck. Once inside, he watched in the rear view mirror while Matt hooked up and raised the old Blazer onto the flatbed. In minutes, they were on the road back to town.

Back at the Sheriff's Station in Nogales, Chance went down to the garage and signed out a new vehicle from the department's herd. The young deputy in charge of the vehicle inventory handed over the keys to a brand new, sleek black Dodge Ram 1500 4X4 extended cab pickup truck with a Hemi engine and all the bells and whistles. As Chance climbed aboard the black chrome and steel giant, he had to admit she was a beautiful mount. She even had that new truck smell that was almost intoxicating to breathe in. It took him a while to find all of the controls to maneuver the big beast, but he found himself thinking she was a sharp, sleek, smooth and fast beauty, like a wild mustang just caught from the faraway hills and culled from the herd to become his new, trusty stead—albeit only a temporary one, until his old Blazer was fixed.

The sun was sinking toward the horizon, so Chance decided to head toward Tubac and his Tuesday evening ritual of a silent meditation class at the Tubac Buddhist Meditation Center to calm his heart and mind. He had been going to the Empty Brush Sangha, housed in Virginia Hall's old painting studio, since it opened several years earlier. He truly looked forward to his weekly Tuesday and Friday evening sessions with the group of free and kindred souls that belonged to and had practiced Zen and Tibetan Buddhism for the last twenty or so years together. Before moving to Virginia Hall's old painting studio, the small group of devotees had gathered and meditated together in an apartment across from the old Tubac cemetery.

Chance's interest in Zen Buddhism had begun back in college, where he majored in criminal justice sciences and minored in philosophy. He had always been drawn to Eastern philosophies and religion, along with American Indian philosophy and religion. The two cultures had much in common with each other, and he could always relate to the similarities in both philosophies, as they were both very much grounded in the principles of nature and the natural world.

Chance had always found his church and his spirituality to manifest itself most strongly in the out-of-doors, specifically, in the wildness of the mountains and desert of the American West. He believed in God as the Creator of all things, but his strongest thoughts and inner passions resonated more within the natural world and the circular pattern of life that he could never find within the physical walls of any traditional church. Chance had found other religions and philosophies to be too rigid and too false for his own tastes and understanding. He had experienced in his life that most of the people who belonged to the more traditional religions were eventually discovered and exposed as utter frauds, fakes, and hypocrites. He would see them sitting in the first pew in church every Sunday, listening to the Gospel of the Lord, and these same people would be found completely disregarding these same teachings and beliefs of their faiths the rest of the week. Inside the walls of their churches they were devout Christians. Once outside again in the real world they were evil back-stabbers and hypocrites who had no genuine faith in God or their fellow man.

Inside the sangha, the Chinese bell rang three times. Chance sat cross-legged on his pillow on the floor, closed his eyes, and began his practice of calming his thoughts and stilling his mind, like a crystal clear pool of a natural spring without as much as a tiny ripple of disturbance above or below its surface. He visualized a clear and empty consciousness, devoid of the turmoil, stress, and anxiety that crept into his outer world constantly but couldn't penetrate his inner self, mind, heart, or soul during his meditation session.

During these sessions he would meditate on everything and nothing for forty-five minutes, until the bell rang once more to peacefully and tranquilly announce the end of the session. Then he would sometimes engage in friendly small talk with his fellow practitioners if he felt the need, or slowly and silently make his way out of the Meditation Center and drive home to Sonoita.

Tonight, with his spirit quieted and the windows of the truck rolled all the way down, he gulped in the fresh desert and mountain air, clearing his lungs, his heart, and his mind of all the bad karma in his county and his world. He pulled into his driveway at the ranch, ready to spend another peaceful and relaxing night with his wife, his dog, and his horses. In the morning, he would be revived and refreshed to reenter the harsh, brutal realities of the world once again, to fulfill his obligations and duties to the citizenry of Santa Cruz County as a modern-day lawman and peaceful warrior to a free and just society.

Chance's slumber was, once again, interrupted by the annoying sound of his cell phone ringing. He reached over to pick up his phone plugged into its battery charger on the nightstand, and he glanced at the glowing red digits of his alarm clock: 2:15. Still half asleep and groggy, he answered his phone and was greeted by a familiar voice on the other end of the line.

"Sorry to wake you, Sheriff. This is Deputy Graves. I'm afraid to tell you we've discovered another cold one."

"I hope you're talking about beer and not another dead body, Graves?"

"Sorry, sir, but it's definitely another dead body."

"You've got to be kidding me! We haven't had a murder in this county in five years, and now we have two in two nights?"

"I'm afraid so, sir," Graves said.

"Where and who is it this time?"

"I know this is hard to believe, but it's the same exact thing as last night. I'm driving past last night's crime scene when I see another naked, dead male hanging from the very same Mesquite tree off Kenyon Ranch Road and I-19 in Tubac. Just like the first one last night, it's an Indian, and he's got his penis and testicles cut off and stuffed in his mouth. I swear, it's like déjà vu all over again, Sheriff. This shit is startin' to get a little spooky."

"All right, Graves, just calm down, stay there, secure the scene—and don't touch anything. You know the drill. I'll be there in twenty minutes."

"You got it, Boss," answered the deputy.

What the hell is happening in this county? Chance wondered. He got dressed, gave his wife a peck on the lips, stepped into his brand spanking new Dodge 1500 pickup truck, and sped away toward the crime scene once again.

He took in the scene: in every detail it was a complete replica of the surreal scene from last night, all the way down to Deputy Graves eating his lunch out of a paper bag, its contents spread out across the hood of his squad car. The only difference seemed to be tonight's sandwich was peanut butter and jelly instead of ham and cheese.

"We've got to stop meeting like this," Chance drawled, "or people are going to start to talk. You've got the luck of an upside down horseshoe shoved up your ass, Graves."

"Quite the coincidence, huh Chief?" Graves said around a big bite of his sandwich.

"Graves, what did I tell you about calling me chief?" Chance yelled, suddenly fuming. He shouldn't let this clown's mistakes get to him, but they always did, especially at 0245. "Again, do I look like a damn Indian chief to you?"

"Ah, no sir. I'm sorry, Chief... I mean, Sheriff. Sheriff Colt, sir. You are definitely Sheriff Colt and in no way do you have any resemblance to an Indian chief, sir. My apologies for being such a dumbass, Sheriff."

Chance glared at his deputy, waved him off, and walked toward the crime scene, all the while attempting to regain his composure. "Graves, just call out the M.E. and have him meet us here. Then sit in your car, write your report, and leave me alone. I'll get Detective Montoya on the horn and we'll clean up this damn mess one more time. Just do what I say and stay the hell out of my way until Detective Montoya gets here. And quit eating that sandwich in front of a dead body. Have some damn respect for the deceased. What kind of an idiot gets hungry while looking at a mutilated, bloody, naked corpse hanging from a tree?"

Deputy Graves swallowed the remainder of his sandwich and began to answer, but Chance put up his hand to stop him. "Never mind; I don't want to know. Just get in your car and write your damn report for Detective Montoya. And get your damn peanut butter and jelly sandwich out of my damn sight right now. Got it?"

The deputy slunk away, and Chance turned his full attention to the crime scene. He shone his flashlight on the dead body and immediately saw the howling wolf tattoo on the deceased's upper right arm and the ring finger missing from his left hand.

"Damn it!" he said aloud. "This shit is starting to piss me off." He reached in his pocket for his cell phone and called Alexis and Black Chief to give them the news of the latest murder that would also ruin their peaceful night's slumber.

Detective Montoya was the first to arrive on the scene. She took one look and said, "It looks like we've got a damn serial killer on the loose in our county, Chance."

"Appears that way, doesn't it?" replied Chance with a frown. "Let's start processing the scene. Graves is in his car writing his report for you, and the M.E. is on his way. Agent Black Chief should be here momentarily. The deceased looks like another member of the Shadow Wolves by the tattoo on his right arm. Do you recognize him?"

"No," answered Alexis, "but I don't work with ICE agents much."

"Me neither," said Chance. "They usually stay exclusively on the rez. I don't know why these two guys got lured away, both to the exact same location two nights in a row." He lowered his flashlight to check the ground under the body and gave a grunt. "Huh! We even have another bloody eagle feather on the ground under this guy's feet."

With that, the sheriff and the detective silently and solemnly went to work on the crime scene, looking for some clues or answers to the mysterious deaths.

Agent Black Chief soon pulled up in his red pickup and quietly walked up to the scene with a somber expression on his face. After shaking hands with the sheriff and the detective, he stated without any hesitation, "That's Jim Walking Horse, another of my men. What the hell is happening to my unit of Shadow Wolves?"

"Looks like we've got a serial killer on our hands, John." Alexis shook her head, her eyebrows raised. "I've never seen anything like this before. It's bizarre beyond words."

"Why and how are your men being lured so far off the reservation, and then being so brutally and sadistically murdered?" asked Chance.

"I wish I had an answer to that, Chance," said Black Chief. "My guys appear to be involved in something way over their heads. We've pissed somebody off, that's for sure. It's got to be a Mexican drug cartel taking revenge on my unit or trying to wipe us out altogether. I'll find out if Jim Walking Horse and Billy Big Bear were working the same case or similar cases. Obviously, there's got to be a connection between these two and their murders."

Mike Munoz, the evidence technician, arrived wearing a look of disgust. And soon after, Dr. Patel showed up to take the corpse to the county morgue to begin his tests and autopsy investigation. Chance knew "Doctor Death" would notify him within twenty-four to forty-eight hours after his test results were completed on the cause of death. However, everyone present at the murder scene was willing to bet the results would be the same cause as the first death: roofies in the bloodstream and a broken neck and asphyxiation, caused by the hanging.

A couple of hours later, as the sun began its brilliant rise above the eastern horizon, Detective Montoya, Agent Black Chief, and Sheriff Colt were combing the crime scene in a circular fashion, about three hundred yards from the hanging tree. They found the same exact evidence that was found after the first murder: no finger prints, both small and large boot prints, 4X4 pickup truck tire tracks, a bloody eagle feather, and a cut-off and missing ring finger from the victim's left hand.

They wrapped up their work at the scene around 0900 hours and headed to a local café for breakfast. It would give them a chance to talk over what they had so far as theories and evidence for the two identical murders. Besides, they were all starving and needed coffee.

After breakfast was over and their discussion of the cases completed, Black Chief headed back to the reservation and his ICE office to see if he could find a connection between what his two recently deceased agents had been working on, and to notify and interview Jim Walking Horse's wife and next of kin. Detective Montoya drove into town again to canvas the local Tubac bar and restaurant owners and employees, to see if Walking Horse had recently visited any of the establishments and to ask about the people he might have been seen with.

Chance drove home to take a shower, change into his uniform, and head back out to the crime scene with his dog for one more look around. Then he would drive into the office in Nogales to begin another long, tedious day of work. He had meetings today with the mayor of Nogales and the city attorney, and then a never-ending pile of paperwork to catch up on at the office—just another day of meetings and politics, the part of the job he hated the most and looked forward to the least.

Chance was a lawman, not a politician. He hated shaking hands, kissing babies, and the pomp and circumstance of being an elected public official, but it was something he had to do, no matter how much he despised this part of the job. After all, to keep his job, he had to keep the politicians and the county citizenry satisfied and happy, regardless of the fact that he had more important things to do. Especially now that he had what appeared to be a serial killer on the loose and was about to be bombarded with news crews and federal agents invading and inundating his county and his staff with questions about the recent murders of two federal ICE agents that occurred on his watch and in his jurisdiction.

Chapter Five

After a hot shower, Chance left his home again and took William Shakespeare along to the scene of the two recent murders. Sometimes, Chance believed, Shakespeare's dog senses could pick up and find evidence that was initially overlooked by the two-legged police. A dog's heightened sense of smell, sight, and hearing could sometimes help him locate additional clues and evidence overlooked by humans. Chance also received some helpful assistance from his ever-present spirit guide, the long-dead Sheriff White.

It was about 1100 hours when Chance pulled up to the crime scene once again. Shakespeare appeared to enjoy the new ride and made himself at home sitting shotgun and upright through the half hour ride in the new Dodge 1500 pickup. He even seemed to deeply breathe in the luxury of that "new truck" smell.

"Don't get too used to it, my friend," Chance said, giving his dog's left ear a good scratch. "I'll be getting the Blazer back from the shop later today."

Shakespeare appeared to look down his long black nose in disapproval and disappointment at Chance after hearing this news; as if to say, "Are you kidding me? We're riding high and in style in this brand new black beauty, and you want to go back to that old Chevy? Sometimes you humans really disappoint me."

Chance opened the driver's side door, and Shakespeare bounded up and over his master to be the first one out of the truck. He followed his nose and ran straight to the dried, bloodstained ground underneath the mesquite tree, appearing to be sniffing for clues that might help solve the case. Chance got out of the truck, shut the door, and leaned against the hood and front bumper, patiently watching his hunting dog investigate the surrounding area.

It's definitely Mexican drug runners who done this, said the ghost of Sheriff White. *No doubt in my mind.*

"Wait a minute. Yesterday you said you were sure it was the Apaches," Chance challenged his ghost.

I changed my mind. A man's got a right to change his mind, especially a dead man.

"You change your mind so damn often, you sound more like a woman talking than a man," quipped Chance. He mulled over the dead sheriff's words and began to work his mind through the multitude of possible scenarios as to how these two murders could have taken place.

Chance was momentarily shaken out of his deep thoughts when he heard Shakespeare bark and saw the dog run behind a thick stand of foothill palo verde trees about two hundred yards away. He could tell by the sound of

Shakespeare's bark that he meant business and therefore must have found something to raise his dander.

Chance ran to his dog and the stand of trees as fast as his fifty-year-old legs would take him over the uneven terrain. When he got to the opposite side of the grove of trees, Shakespeare was guarding and slowly closing in on two young male Hispanics hiding under the trees. Chance drew his .40 caliber Glock and gave the order in Spanish for the men to come out from under the trees with their hands held high so he could see them. Shakespeare was slowly moving in for his attack when Chance called him off and ordered him to stand down. The two Hispanics emerged looking dirty, tired, and frightened as they moved into a clearing with their outstretched arms held over their heads.

Chance held his Glock steady as he identified himself as a lawman and performed a body search of both men to make sure they carried no weapons. Finding none, he handcuffed the larger of the two males first and ordered him to lie face down on the ground. He then commanded the smaller man to lie face down on the ground next to the first man and handcuffed his hands behind his back as well.

With Shakespeare standing guard over the men, Chance pointed his pistol at both men with his left hand while he called into his radio to dispatch with his right hand.

"Santa Cruz dispatch from Unit 10."

"Go ahead, Unit 10." The familiar voice of his day shift dispatcher, Shirley, responded immediately.

"I'm at the murder scene in Tubac from the last two nights, and I need backup. I have two Hispanic males in custody. Can you send any available units for assistance?"

"10-4 Unit 10. I have two deputies, Unit 25 and Unit 27, in your vicinity and en route to your location."

"Shirley, call in the Border Patrol also. From the looks of them, I think they're illegal crossers."

"10-4 Unit 10. I am TX'ing BP now."

Within ten minutes two Santa Cruz County deputies had arrived at the scene, along with two Border Patrol Chevy Tahoe units. By this time, Shakespeare was back underneath the palo verdes barking out his latest find. The discovery turned out to be two heavy backpacks stuffed full of what appeared to be marijuana bricks.

Chance spoke with his deputies and the two Border Patrol agents, instructing all of them about interrogating the two males in custody. He made it clear that they needed to be questioned not only about being illegal immigrants and being in possession of the marijuana, but also about possibly witnessing the two recent murders at the very location where they had been hiding.

"They both have carpet squares glued to the bottoms of their shoes, so as not to leave footprints," Chance said, "so I don't like them for being responsible for the murders—they wouldn't have left any tracks or footprints in the sand wearing the carpet. But question them anyway as to how long they've been hiding here and if they may have seen anything in regard to the murders. I don't think we would have missed them during the initial search because we were all over these palo verdes, but ask them anyway just to make sure."

Chance returned to his truck with Shakespeare and gave the dog a treat and some fresh water as his reward for his good police work and a job well done.

After an hour of questioning, it became apparent that the two Hispanics were illegal crossers and drug mules being paid to hump the two loads of marijuana across the border for future sale and distribution in the United States. It also became apparent that they had just recently arrived to this location, as Chance had thought, and hid under the trees when they saw Chance's truck pull up. These two "wets" had no knowledge of or involvement with the murders of the Shadow Wolf Agents—lucky for them. It just happened to be their bad luck, karma, chance and circumstance that they chose a route into the United States and Santa Cruz County that just happened to be in the vicinity of the two recent murders. These weren't high-level drug cartel members, but two lowly grunts being paid to run some dope across the border in exchange for their freedom and the potential of a new start and a new life in El Norte.

With this information obvious and apparent, the Border Patrol agents took custody of the two illegal crossers and their booty of marijuana. Chance and his two deputies could be on their merry way. Even though the Border Patrol agents would get credit for the bust, Chance knew it was Shakespeare's good police work that caught the bad guys; all in a day's work for Sheriff Colt and his trusty sidekick, William Shakespeare.

Chance was running late for his meetings in Nogales with the mayor and city attorney, so he flipped on his lights and hightailed it in the new Dodge 1500 to Nogales and his station. He had to admit that the truck was impressive, with its Hemi engine propelling him and his dog comfortably along I-19 at a constant speed of 110 miles per hour.

When they reached Nogales, he dropped Shakespeare off at the station, leaving him in Shirley's capable hands. The dog sprawled under her desk at her feet, perfectly content. Unable to delay any longer, Chance headed for the mayor's office for his meeting and to perform his political and civic duties.

At around 1700 hours, after returning to his office and finishing off some long-overdue paperwork, Chance checked in by phone with Alexis and Black Chief to find out if they had any new information or leads regarding the two Shadow Wolf cases. The answers were negative, so he headed over to vehicle inventory with William Shakespeare. It was time to return the new Dodge truck and pick up his repaired Blazer.

At inventory, he turned over the keys of the Dodge to the deputy and asked for a ride to Matt's Towing. The deputy climbed into the cab and wrinkled his nose.

"Hey, it smells like wet dog in here, and there's black hair and saliva all over the front and back seats," he said, looking at Shakespeare with anger and disgust. "Who's gonna clean up all of this black hair and dog drool?"

"Why, I guess you are," replied the sheriff with a grin. "After all, you're the vehicle inventory deputy, aren't you?"

The deputy swung the big truck out onto the highway and headed for the towing yard. "Yeah, but I ain't no kennel cleaner for big black slobs."

"Be careful with your words now; you sound a lot like you're racial profiling at this point. That could get you into some serious trouble." Chance gave his dog a left-ear scratch, and Shakespeare responded by licking his face. "I would apologize to Deputy Shakespeare, if I were you. After all, this brave and hard-working police dog made a big drug bust today. What did you do today to top that, Deputy?"

"Nothing, I guess," answered the inventory deputy. "The highlight of my day will be cleaning up the mess Super Dog left behind."

"That's Deputy Shakespeare, to you. Anyway, thanks for the ride." Chance hopped out with Shakespeare as soon as the truck came to a stop in Matt's parking lot. "Deputy

Shakespeare and I appreciate your hospitality and your hard work. Now get back to the station and clean up this filthy truck pronto. Our department has a high reputation and image to uphold, and I wouldn't want a dirty, smelly, unkempt vehicle to tarnish that image. It shows a lack of professionalism." Chance gave his deputy a friendly wink, but the man just rolled his eyes.

"Have a good night, Sheriff—of course, that goes for Deputy Shakespeare too," the deputy said. Chance shut the passenger door, and the deputy gunned the engine and roared out of the parking lot in a cloud of dust.

Chance found Matt inside the repair shop office. "Hey, Matt, how's my Blazer doing?"

"Oh hey, Sheriff. She's as good as new." Matt offered the sheriff a hearty handshake and a smile. "I mean, if it was 1989."

"She's an oldie but a goodie, you know. We've traveled many miles and many roads together, me and this truck. Thanks for fixing her up again for me."

"You're welcome. That's what I do, you know—I fix things."

"Me too, Matt. In a way, we have kind of the same calling in life," Chance said, taking the keys from Matt and signing off on the invoice. "Only you fix vehicles and I fix people. Or we try to, anyway. Until we meet again, Matt. You take care of yourself."

"You take care too. I have a feeling we'll be meeting again soon, when you're broke down in the middle of nowhere."

"That's what friends are for, right?" Chance and Shakespeare jumped into the old Blazer and started her up. With a final wave to Matt, they headed off into the setting sun.

Chapter Six

Sonoita and the ranch lay just ahead in the gathering dusk. Chance felt dead-on-his-feet tired; life tired. After another busy night and day investigating a second murder, he felt like going home and sleeping for about two weeks straight. Maybe that would relieve his physical, emotional, and mental exhaustion, all due to his profession and decades on the job. Sometimes Chance felt that his career was slowly draining the life out of him, if not physically killing him.

He had just turned off the main road and into his mile-long ranch driveway when his Motorola radio crackled. *What now?* Chance wondered.

"Santa Cruz dispatch to any available units, we have a 10-10 in progress at the Steak Out Restaurant & Saloon at 3200 S. Sonoita Highway. The manager called it in—he's having trouble with a group of Hell's Angels."

"Ah, hell's bells!" Chance yelled. "Just what I need—gettin' in the middle of a brawl." He picked up his radio. "Dispatch, this is Unit 10. I'm five minutes from that location and en route."

"10-4, Unit 10." The police radio went silent, which meant no other units were in the area.

"Shit!" Chance said, looking sideways at his dog. "It looks like you and me are the whole cavalry, Shake and Bake." He backed out of his driveway, hit the lights and siren, and proceeded to peel some expensive rubber from his rear off-road tires.

He arrived to the Steak Out in just under five minutes, making good time in the old Chevy Blazer. Upon pulling into the parking lot of the restaurant and saloon, his eyes fixed on approximately thirty Harley Davidson motorcycles parked side-by-side across the entire front of the establishment. Not a soul was outside, so he knew the fight and the odds were clearly against him and Shakespeare, as they both ran from the truck to the restaurant's front door.

The Steak Out was well-known locally for great steak, barbecued ribs and burgers, and what could be, at times, a rowdy bar frequented by locals, cowboys, tourists, and bikers travelling through southern Arizona. Walking inside, the restaurant was situated on the left side of the building; the bar was on the right.

As Chance entered with Shakespeare, he immediately heard and saw a mass of bikers in the bar wearing their Hell's Angels leather jackets, vests, t-shirts, and colors, along with displaying their trademark tattoos and nasty attitudes. Chance could see the bar manager, Cody, and a white male bartender standing behind the bar with baseball bats held high and looks of firm defiance on their red faces.

Chance quickly decided to make a grand entrance and a bold statement to draw the immediate attention of the boisterous crowd. He was carrying his fully loaded Winchester model 1894 30-30 long rifle—a family heirloom and one of his few prized possessions. He cocked a 150 grain three-inch lead and brass round into the firing chamber, pulled back the hammer with his thumb, aimed the barrel at the wooden wall behind the bar, and gently pulled the trigger.

The loud and unmistakable explosion of the round splintering into the back wall created the effect Chance had desired, and only a mere two seconds after the shot, the entire crowd and room were so quiet, you could've heard a pin drop. However, instead of dropping a pin, Chance ejected the spent shell and chambered another round. The only sound now audible in the place was of the ejected empty brass shell hitting and rolling across the floor and underneath a high-top table.

Chance then leveled the Winchester at the silent bikers as the whole room full of eyes turned toward him and stared. Not wanting to waste such a fine dramatic moment, Chance spoke aloud his thoughts, using his best Clint Eastwood impression.

"The next shot won't hit the wall. The next shot will be fired at one of your heads, which will then splatter brain matter all over the room like an exploding pumpkin. Do I have everyone's full and complete attention?"

No one in the place moved or uttered a sound.

"My name is Sheriff Chance Colt, and I'm the law in this county. I'm not sure what the trouble is, but I'm here to tell you that it ends now. Comprende, everyone?" Chance slowly pointed the rifle from one head to another among the crowd of bikers. Then he turned to the bar manager. "Cody, what seems to be the problem?"

"We was just havin' a little disagreement with these fine patrons over the payment of their bar tab, Sheriff."

"What's the disagreement about?" Chance continued to scan the crowd of bikers with his Winchester, paying particular attention to everyone's hands and eyes.

"They're sayin' I overcharged them for their beer," Cody answered.

"Well, did you?"

"Did I what?" Cody countered, looking a little confused and bewildered.

"Did you overcharge these ladies and gentlemen on their tab?"

"Why, no—I even gave 'em a ten percent discount off their total tab, just to be neighborly." Cody's voice shook slightly.

"Well then ladies and gentlemen, it appears it's time to settle up and pay your bill and start making your way out of my county before something unfortunate happens," stated the sheriff, with a look that meant all business.

A big, bald-headed biker slowly took one step forward toward the sheriff and began to speak. William Shakespeare immediately stepped up to meet him with a low, guttural growl and bared teeth that also clearly meant business. Shakespeare's demeanor even slightly surprised Chance.

"We don't want no trouble with you or your dog, Sheriff. What's his name, anyway?" the bald biker asked Chance as he put up his hands and anxiously looked down at Shakespeare's exposed fangs.

"His name is William Shakespeare, like the poet and playwright. If he likes you, you can call him William or even

Bill, but it appears to me that he don't like you much, Mister. To be on the safe side, I'd advise you to call him Deputy Shakespeare. Then slowly back away from him and pay your bill to Cody. And make sure you tip Cody and his barkeep well, as I'm sure their service to you and your friends was top notch, and they deserve a little something for the effort."

Big Baldy smiled and then laughed, but Chance didn't return the niceties; he kept his rifle pointed at Baldy's head with a stern demeanor. Shakespeare continued to growl and show his teeth, and he even began drooling, his saliva dripping on the wooden floor. *Shake and Bake looks like Cujo, the Hound from Hell,* thought Chance.

Big Baldy ambled slowly over to the bar, picked up the tab, looked at it, and set it back down. Then he reached into his pants pocket, removed a wad of bills, and pulled out three $100 bills. "Will this cover our tab and the tip, barkeep?" he inquired.

"It sure will," answered Cody, still gripping his baseball bat. "Me and my bartender are much obliged."

"Good," Big Baldy responded. He turned to the crowd of silent bikers and said quietly and firmly, "Hell's Angels, let's leave this fine establishment and be on our way. We got a long ride to Laughlin ahead of us."

"You goin' to bike week in Laughlin, Nevada?" Chance said.

"Yes we are, Sheriff," answered Big Baldy, "so if you and Deputy Shakespeare don't mind, we'll be leavin' about now and be on our way."

"Don't mind at all," said Chance. "As a matter of fact, I'd prefer it before my deputy loses his temper and lets loose on one of you. He's got a long tail but a short fuse, if you know what I mean."

Big Baldy smiled and said he and his friends understood what the sheriff meant loud and clear. "You have a good evening, Sheriff," said Big Baldy, as he slowly led his Hell's Angels out single file past the Sheriff and into the parking lot.

"You too, ladies and gentlemen. Y'all drive safely now, you hear?" said the sheriff politely, as he moved his rifle to rest on his shoulder and instructed Shakespeare to stand down and at ease. "Have fun at bike week. I've been to Laughlin for bike week in my younger days. We always had a great time. Y'all do the same," said the sheriff with a big, fake Hollywood smile on his face, as he followed the gang out to the parking lot. "I used to ride a Harley myself."

Big Baldy asked, "Were you one of us back then, Sheriff?"

"No," Chance answered. "I've always been a lone wolf, myself."

Chance spotted three Santa Cruz County sheriff's deputy trucks pulling into the parking lot. The bikers saw them too, and they peacefully started their Harleys, smiled, waved, and slowly drove west out of town. And, Chance hoped, out of his county.

After the gang of Hell's Angels had ridden out of sight, Chance took in a deep breath and let out a big sigh of relief. He turned to his deputies and said aloud, "Well, better late than never, I guess."

"Sorry, sir. We got here as soon as we could," Deputy Graves said. The three deputies nodded in unison.

"I have to hand it to you, Graves. Your timing is impeccable, as always." Chance patted his deputy on the back with a smile. "Thanks for covering my six." He sat down on the wooden bench in front of the Steak Out, called over his dog, and gave him a good petting. "Thanks, partner," he told

Shakespeare, as the dog appeared to let out his own sigh of relief. "That was some kind of play-acting on your part. You almost had me convinced you're a mean son of a bitch. The spit and foaming at the mouth at the end was over the top, though."

William Shakespeare seemed to be smiling as he lapped up the praise of his best friend and partner.

Cody, his bartender, and all of his waitresses came outside to thank Sheriff Colt and Shakespeare personally. Several of them laughed nervously for a few minutes before they all piled back inside to get back to work.

Cody rested a hand on the sheriff's shoulder and asked with a hint of sarcasm, "So, you gonna pay for the repair of that bullet hole you put in my wall?"

"Nah, I think it gives the place more character. I'd leave it as it is as a conversation piece; it's just another bullshit bar story you can tell your customers about. It gives the place more of a Wild West look and flavor. The tourists will eat it up."

"I agree," Cody said with a laugh. "And thanks again. For a couple of minutes there, I thought we were all gonna die tonight. Thanks for everything you do, Sheriff."

"No thanks necessary, Cody, just doin' my job."

Cody reached out to grasp the sheriff's hand before going back inside the bar, leaving Chance and Shakespeare sitting alone in the dark of the night. Chance slowly unloaded the six unfired rounds from his Winchester rifle and patted his dog with his shaking hands, as the adrenalin slowly dissipated in his body. When both man and dog were sufficiently calm once again, Chance and Shakespeare got into the cab of the Blazer, happy to have survived another day in this modern world gone mad.

Chance drove toward home that night with the realization he had dodged a bullet again—literally. Only a few years earlier, during another Laughlin bike week, all hell had broken loose inside Harrah's Casino Hotel, right on the gaming floor. Two rival biker gangs, the Hell's Angels and the Mongols, had started an argument that quickly escalated into an all-out knife and gun battle on the casino floor.

Caught right in the middle of the Old West shootout were hundreds of innocent bystanders and patrons who quickly scattered, dashing for cover. When the fighting ended, two Hell's Angels and one Mongol gang member were dead. The Mongol had been stabbed to death, the two Hell's Angels had been shot to death, and at least thirteen others had been injured in the mayhem.

Chance had run into the Hell's Angels and other motorcycle gangs on a few occasions in his career, and he knew from those experiences that the best thing a lawman can do is immediately set the tone and take control of the crowd and the situation before the biker gangs have a chance to react or initiate violence. Violence can be golden in a tense situation, similar to the one he had just encountered, as long as the law enforcement officer acts quickly to get the upper hand by initiating the violence.

As Chance turned the Blazer into his long driveway for the second time that night, he took another couple of deep breaths to calm himself. He parked the truck in front of the house, and he and his dog exited the vehicle. Chance gave Shakespeare some time to relieve himself, as he stood on his front porch looking out at the clear, calm, starry night.

He smiled to himself. Funny how the outside world could always appear so calm while a person's inner world could be in complete turmoil and chaos. Sheriff Colt and "Super Dog" then entered the front door of his peaceful log home and instantly transformed themselves into calm, cool, and collected old Chance and Shake and Bake.

Sarah stood at the stove making dinner for the three of them, her hair in a messy knot on top of her head and her jeans dusted with flour. She greeted her husband with a smile and her dog with a gentle pat on the head before they went to the table to enjoy dinner together.

Sarah had learned early in their marriage not to ask Chance about his day of law enforcement duties and keeping the peace, so they talked lightly and calmly about Sarah's day, the weather, the horses, the ranch, friends and family—anything but Chance's job. It was his time to shut out the real world and enter into his peaceful other world, if even for a short while, so he could relax, rejuvenate and reenergize his heart, his mind, and his soul.

After dinner Chance and Sarah started a small fire in the stone fireplace and settled in for a quiet night of reading and talking. Shakespeare sprawled between their two rocking chairs in front of the warm fire, sound asleep.

Around 2200 hours, Chance went out to the barn to check on the horses. Finding them peaceful, docile, well-fed, and watered, he held a short conversation with both Butch and Sundance before bidding them a good night. In bed and sleeping soundly by 2300 hours, with his wife and dog at his side, Chance slept for eight hours straight until he woke up without the need for an alarm clock.

For once, Chance thought, *it was good to not be awakened in the middle of the night by my cell phone delivering bad news.*

He got out of bed, drank some hot coffee with Sarah, shaved, showered, and set out for another day of fighting the good fight and upholding the law of the land and the Code of the West.

Chapter Seven

"Sorry it's taken me so long to get back to you, Sheriff," said Dr. Patel, "but it's been a busy week for people dying in our county."

"No problem," Chance said. It was around 0900 when he picked up the phone to get the M.E.'s autopsy results for Jim Walking Horse. "I suppose more deaths are good job security for guys like you." He waited for Patel to laugh, but instead the phone went silent for several long seconds. The good doctor didn't seem to find Chance's gallows humor funny. "I'm just kidding, Doc," added Chance.

"I don't find death amusing, especially when it's a homicide."

"Right. Sometimes in our line of work we just have to joke about things like that so it doesn't get to us. So, I take it the victim is still dead?" Chance said with a grin that the doctor couldn't see, just to get another rise out of him.

"Of course the victim is still dead."

"That's good to know. Just give me the autopsy results, and I'll stop kidding with you and let you get back to work on all your other recently deceased friends."

"Very well. My apologies. I am East Indian, and I'm not sure I understand your American sense of humor."

"Gotcha, Doc. Just cut to the chase."

"What chase?" Dr. Patel sounded confused.

"Just give me the results of your autopsy, if you don't mind."

"By all means. Jim Walking Horse had the same drug in his bloodstream as your first victim: Rohypnol or roofies, the tranquilizer. However, the cause of death was asphyxiation and a broken neck from the hanging. I also believe his genitals and left ring finger were cut off, once again, postmortem. No finger prints or physical evidence of any kind that would identify the assailant were found on the body or at the scene. You have an angry and sadistic killer out there on the loose."

"Thanks, Doc. Anything else?" Chance looked up from his phone just in time to see six nearly identical-looking white men, with crew cuts and dressed in black suits, white dress shirts, red ties, and black sunglasses, walk into his office lobby in single file and stop in front of Shirley's desk.

"Hey, listen, I need to let you go," he told the M.E. hastily. "The men in black just showed up, and it looks like I have to entertain the troops." Chance hung up on Doctor Death, as Patel was still in mid-sentence saying his formal goodbye.

Chance walked briskly out of his office and intercepted the men before they could start interrogating his dispatcher.

"Nice suits and sunglasses, guys," he said with a friendly grin. "Did you bring Will Smith and Tommy Lee Jones along for the ride?" Chance saw no reaction at all, so he went on. "You'll be needing those sunglasses here in sunny southern Arizona. That was a smart move on your part."

The first in line of the men in black said, "I'm Special Agent Ryan. We're with the Federal Bureau of Investigation and we're looking for Sheriff Chance Colt."

"Well, it must be your lucky day, Agent Ryan—you've found him. What can I do for you fellas?" Chance was performing his best dumb-county-sheriff impersonation. "We don't get you FBI fellas in these parts very often. Do you mind if I see some identification from all of you gentlemen before we speak in my office?"

"Of course, Sheriff," answered Agent Ryan. "My apologies."

All six men showed their credentials to Sheriff Colt before following him into his office. He politely shook the hand of each man in turn and closed the door behind them. Seven men standing in his office made the space feel small, but he wanted the privacy without the formality of the interrogation room.

"Who is currently in charge of the investigation of the two murdered Shadow Wolves?" Agent Ryan asked.

"Right now, it's kind of a three-headed monster," replied Chance. "My department is coordinating the investigation with the Agent in Charge of the Shadow Wolves unit—ICE Agent John Black Chief. He's been working with one of my detectives, Alexis Montoya, and me."

"Excellent," said Ryan. "We'll be taking over the investigation from here since it's a federal case and falls under federal jurisdiction. I'm sure you understand the protocol."

"I sure do," said Chance. "Both cases are all yours. Do you need anything from my department at this point?"

"Not a thing other than your department's cooperation."

Ryan stared blankly at the sheriff for almost two full minutes without anyone speaking. Chance finally broke the uncomfortable silence. "Do you guys want a copy of our case files? Will you need the location where the murders took place?"

"Yes, that would be helpful. Thank you. That will be all for now." Ryan took a step toward the office door, and the other five federal agents lined up single file behind him.

Chance paused and gave the feds a once-over. "Are you sure you brought enough guys, Agent Ryan?" he asked with a grin. Again, Ryan just stood there and looked blankly at the sheriff in silence. Chance turned back toward the door, rolled his eyes, and said, "I'll get the files and make you a copy, and I'll write down the address of the crime scene for you." Chance kept his inner thoughts to himself—*Would you like me to wipe your asses for you too?* "And I'll give you directions and draw you a map."

"That won't be necessary," said Ryan. "We have GPS."

"Oh yeah, GPS." Chance smiled and tried not to laugh. "I forgot you federal guys have all the new-fangled gadgets to work with."

He came back to his office a few minutes later with copies of the dead men's files, as well as a hand-drawn map and directions to the murder scene. He handed Agent Ryan his business card and added, "Call me if you get lost. Oh, and make sure you say hello to Will Smith and Tommy Lee Jones for me, okay? I always loved the movie *Men in Black.*"

The six feds just stood there and stared at the sheriff like a litter of lost puppies.

"The exit is that way, gentlemen." Chance opened his office door and pointed to the front door of the Sheriff's Station. The agents exited the building, still walking in single file. "Sharp as razor blades," he commented to Shirley. "And God help this country if they're the best we have to protect us when the shit hits the fan."

Shirley gave a laugh that sounded more like a snort, and Chance walked back into his office and closed the door behind him. He picked up the phone and called Alexis and Black Chief to find out if they had any new information on either case and to suggest they meet for lunch to discuss the investigations and the newest chain of events involving the feds.

"I want to solve both of these cases before they do," he told them. "We have a four-day head start on them already, and we'll get two more days by using tomorrow and Sunday."

"Why do you think we have Saturday and Sunday on them too?" Alexis asked him.

"Everybody in law enforcement knows the FBI doesn't work weekends. That's why they never solve any real crimes—they're just paper-pushing bureaucrats, not real lawmen. Since today is Friday, they won't even start their investigation until Monday morning. I'd like to have it solved by then. Let's meet for lunch at the Cow Palace in Amado at 1100 hours, discuss what we have so far, and go from there."

After he got off the horn with the agent and detective, Chance looked up from his desk just as a whole new group of strangers, both men and women, walked into the lobby of the Sheriff's Station and surrounded Shirley at her desk. *Jesus, it's turning into a damn circus parade around here today,* he said to himself as he walked out of his office and to the waiting crowd in the lobby. "What can we do for you folks?"

The whole group began to speak at once, and that was Chance's first clue that they were all reporters. There were television and radio crews, along with a couple of newspaper journalists, all asking for an impromptu press conference. Would Sheriff Colt kindly spill the beans regarding the two recent murders of federal law enforcement officers in his county?

News media people love to talk, but Chance raised his hands in front of them to silence the crowd. "I'm not sure who you are and what media agencies you all represent, but we only have one short statement to make and we won't be answering any questions. Then you'll all be asked to leave the premises and let us go back to work and perform our jobs."

Someone in the crowd tried to ask a direct question, but he cut them off. "Quiet, please. All I have to say is this: Our official statement is that we have had two unfortunate occurrences happen in Santa Cruz County in the last few days. The result was the deaths of two Department of Immigration and Customs Enforcement Agents, known as Shadow Wolves, an elite American Indian unit of ICE agents who work exclusively on the Tohono O'odham Indian reservation protecting the U.S. border with Mexico on reservation land to prevent drug smuggling and human trafficking onto the reservation and into the U.S.

"A continual and ongoing investigation is being conducted by several federal and local law enforcement organizations at this time in coordination and partnership with each other to investigate these two murders and bring the assailant or assailants into law enforcement custody as soon as possible. That's all we have at this time, and I won't be taking any questions. Thank you for your patience and understanding while we get back to work to solve these cases as quickly as possible. Once we know anything further, you'll be briefed accordingly."

The throng of reporters began asking a barrage of questions all at the same time, directed at Sheriff Colt. He held up his hands again.

"As I stated before, we will answer no questions at this time. I will now have to direct you to leave the building, or you will be arrested by me and my deputies for trespassing. Thank you for your understanding. Now everyone move along and exit the building in an orderly fashion."

Chance and the few deputies who were present then began herding the press people together, like a herd of bawling cattle about to be slaughtered. They quickly ushered the reporters out the door of the building, and Chance closed the door behind them, leaving the media folk standing on the sidewalk outside the station house.

The group dispersed peacefully and quickly back to their vehicles and began driving away and around town, looking for someone or anyone they could interview or get a sound bite from. Chance watched them from the window of his front office as they slowly disappeared. However, he was fully aware that the media are like flies on horses: you can swat them away, but they come right back, once again, to constantly irritate you and your horse.

Chance yelled aloud from his office to his team in the station house, "At this time, absolutely no press interviews allowed. Does everyone understand?"

A chorus of answers in the affirmative sounded out, answering the sheriff's question loud and clear.

"Does anyone have any questions?" Chance inquired. When not a single soul spoke up, he nodded, satisfied. "Good. Let's all get back to work."

Chance whirled on the heels of his cowboy boots and informed Shirley he was leaving to meet Detective Montoya and Agent Black Chief for lunch. "If you need me, call me or radio me. I'll be at the Cow Palace to find out where we currently stand on these two cases. Do you need anything before I leave, Shirley?"

"Only a couple of aspirin for my aching head," she answered. "Those media people are loud talkers."

"Tell me about it. They're all pushy, loud, and obnoxious. If they keep bugging you, you have my permission to lock the front door. I'll talk to you later."

Chance had just merged into the busy main street, heading for the Cow Palace, when he noticed a black Cadillac Escalade pulling into traffic a couple of vehicles behind him. Immediately, he recognized the driver as FBI Agent Ryan, along with one of his generic, non-descript men in black sitting in the passenger seat. The sheriff turned onto the northbound on-ramp of I-19 and settled in for his forty-minute drive to Amado. Mutt and Jeff, in their black Escalade, continued to follow several car lengths behind him.

They stick out like two circus clowns at a rodeo, he thought to himself.

About halfway through his leisurely drive to Amado, Chance decided to pull off to the side of the highway to see what the feds would do. As Chance figured, they pulled to the side of the highway and parked right behind his truck, not trying to be inconspicuous in the least. Chance turned on his flashing lights on the Blazer's light bar, unbuckled his seat belt, exited his vehicle, and slowly walked back with a smile on his face to the passenger side of the Escalade, so as to protect himself from being struck by oncoming traffic.

The federal agent on the passenger side rolled down the window, and Chance leaned in. "Why are you and your partner following me, Agent Ryan?"

"We're gathering intelligence," Ryan answered with a deadpan look on his face.

"You're gathering intelligence," Chance repeated.

"Yes we are, Sheriff," said Ryan.

"Well, if you two geniuses are gathering intelligence, you might as well get yourselves a dump truck," the sheriff stated, "'cause you're gonna need it. You do know that I'm the sheriff of this county, right? What I'm tryin' to get at is, do you guys realize I'm on the same side as you?"

"Yes, we understand that perfectly well. You see, everyone is guilty until proven innocent by us," explained Agent Ryan. "That's our motto."

"That's your motto? That's a good one, Agent; I'll have to remember that, so I can add it to the Code of the West," replied Chance.

"We use a process of elimination when it comes to suspects. It's a technique we learned at Quantico."

"If you're gonna solve this case by the process of elimination, starting with me, you boys are gonna be here for a long while. We use a process down here called 'common sense.' Ever hear of it? It's a technique we learned in kindergarten, when we were five years old. You guys ought to try it sometime."

The agent in the passenger seat coughed into his hand, and Chance could have sworn he heard the word "rube" in the middle of the cough. He chose to ignore it.

"Good luck, gentlemen, and have a nice day," he said, stepping back from the car. "Feel free to follow me until the cows come home, although that may be a long while too, as I don't have any cows. I only have a dog, a horse, and a wife. If you want to follow and interrogate them sometime during your process of elimination, I can introduce you to them all. The dog and horse don't say much, but the wife is a Chatty Cathy who always enjoys company."

He walked back to his truck, shaking his head in amazement at the stupidity of the feds. After that, he ignored them; they could do whatever they liked and it was no skin off his back.

Chance pulled off of I-19 in Amado and parked in the lot at the Cow Palace, waved to the feds when they pulled in behind him, and walked inside to meet Alexis and Black Chief. He had already seen the detective's Dodge Charger and Black Chief's red GMC pickup parked in the lot, so he knew they would be waiting for him. They waved him over to their booth in the back. Chance removed his brown cowboy hat and wiped the sweat from the heat of the day from his brow.

"Alexis, John," he said as he sat down next to his detective.

Right on cue, in came the two federal agents. They settled into a booth several tables away.

"Allow me to introduce my shadows," Chance said, pointing directly at the feds. "That's Agent Mutt and that's Agent Jeff from the FBI. They're using a highly sophisticated law enforcement technique they learned at the FBI academy in Quantico, Virginia. It's called the process of elimination."

"The process of elimination of what?" asked Alexis, chuckling.

"It's how they eliminate suspects and narrow down the field of who committed the crime they're investigating," Chance said with a wry grin. "It's cutting edge federal technology and federal agent philosophy on solving crime."

"So they're following you," Black Chief said seriously, "to eliminate you as a suspect in the Shadow Wolf murders?"

"Yep. You got it, John. They've been shadowing me all morning."

"You've got to be kidding me," Alexis said.

"I wish I was. They'll probably start following you guys next."

All three of them turned and stared in unison at the two federal agents, who were perusing their lunch menus. Black Chief held up his water glass as if to toast the feds; Alexis simply waved hello and smiled. Mutt and Jeff responded by hiding their faces behind their menus.

Must be a hi-tech and sophisticated law enforcement and covert surveillance technique taught at the FBI academy, thought Chance. "Don't worry," he said, "I'll introduce you to them on our way out. They're just kind of timid and shy. In the meantime, let's just ignore them and discuss the cases and what we have so far."

"I interviewed Billy's and Jim's wives and children," said Black Chief. "Obviously, they're all genuinely devastated by the murders. Neither of the wives indicated any kind of marital problems or suspicious behavior. They're both just numb right now." He paused while the waitress poured more coffee in his cup, then he stirred sugar in it. "I also reviewed both Billy's and Jim's work and the cases they were involved in. It didn't appear they were working on anything big or anything in common. They knew each other, of course, and were professional colleagues, but they weren't what I would call close friends. They were just two men living their lives and doing their jobs. There's nothing glaring that sticks out with either one of them. No one can seem to figure out why either man would be found hanging from a tree so far off the rez in Tubac."

Chance nodded. "Thanks, John. How about you, Alexis—do you have anything?"

"As a matter of fact I do. I've spent the last few days talking to every store, bar, and restaurant owner and employee in Tubac and showing them photos of both victims. It turns out Billy was seen a few hours before his death at Elvira's Restaurant & Bar in Tubac, dining and drinking with a young Native woman. He was identified from his photo by both the waitress and bartender. And Jim Walking Horse was observed the next day at Elvira's with the same woman, identified by the same waitress and bartender."

"Good work, Detective." Chance shoveled a chunk of ham and eggs into his mouth and washed it down with coffee.

"It seems," Alexis continued, "that both couples were cordial during their time together at Elvira's, both eating a meal together and consuming several alcoholic beverages."

"What were they drinking?" asked Chance.

"According to both the bartender and the waitress, on both occasions the couples got pretty hammered drinking Long Island iced teas throughout their meals."

"Huh!" Chance said. "Sounds like they were partying pretty hearty with this woman. Did they give you a good description of her?"

"Yes. They both gave the same general description: Native American female, approximately late twenties to early thirties, about five feet four inches tall, weight about one hundred forty to one hundred sixty pounds. She had black hair braided in a single braid down to her waist, dark skin, round face and a big white smile."

"That sounds like any female Indian within a hundred miles of here," Chance remarked.

"Except for one last detail described by both the waitress and bartender," Alexis said. "She had a tattoo on her right upper arm depicting a wolf howling at a full moon."

John Black Chief dropped his water glass on the floor, shattering it into pieces and splattering his jeans. The waitress hustled over to their table with a whisk broom and a towel and cleaned up the spill.

"Would you like another glass of ice water, honey?" asked the waitress.

Black Chief nodded and quietly apologized to the waitress for causing the spill. Chance thought he looked like he was gritting his teeth; a storm of silent rage appeared to be brewing on the agent's face. Chance and Alexis waited patiently for John to speak, but he sat in silence until the waitress brought him a new glass of water. At their table across the restaurant, the two federal agents openly stared at Black Chief.

Once the waitress had left their table, Black Chief took a long sip of his ice water, cleared his throat, and began to speak quietly, with his head down and his eyes staring straight at his full plate of food. "We only have two female Shadow Wolves, and they both match that description: Linda Augustine and Anna Antone," said Black Chief.

"Any vehicle information or description from the waitress or bartender?" asked Chance.

Alexis answered with a quiet, "Yes. They each stated the patrons left both days in a light blue, late seventies, Ford F-150 pickup truck with Arizona license plates."

John Black Chief's face appeared even redder with anger. "That would be Anna Antone's vehicle."

Chance let the information sink in slowly for a moment. He then softly asked John, "Can you obtain a search warrant from the tribal court judge to impound and search the truck and search the residence of Agent Anna Antone?"

"You bet," answered Black Chief, who was barely holding in his anger at this point by continuing to grit his teeth and stare at his lunch plate.

"Let's not jump to conclusions just yet. It could be nothing, John," said Chance. "They may have just been eating lunch together," he said, trying to reassure his friend, but Chance knew he didn't even believe his own words. "If she did it, we'll get a match on the truck tires from the scene and most likely find traces of blood matching both victims' blood in the bed of her truck, no matter how hard she may have tried to clean it up."

"I'm good," said Black Chief, "but I need some fresh air. I'll be waiting outside by my truck. I just need a few minutes to collect myself and my thoughts." Black Chief got up from the table and walked out of the restaurant.

"Holy shit!" said Chance.

"I know," answered Alexis. "I'm sorry to have to be the one to break the news to him like that, but it is what it is. Let's hope both Billy Big Bear and Jim Walking Horse were just having an innocent lunch with their colleague."

"Once we get the search warrants for the truck and house, we'll soon have our answer."

Alexis and Chance got up from the table and went to the front counter to pay the bill. The FBI agents followed both of them with their steely eyes, while staying seated in their booth. Then they quickly got up to pay their bill, as well.

Chance took this opportunity to introduce Detective Alexis Montoya to Special Agent Ryan and his partner. They all shook hands and walked out together to the parking lot, where Chance introduced ICE Agent in Charge John Black Chief to the FBI agents. They both shook hands with Agent Black Chief and exchanged pleasantries. After a brief interlude of small talk among the law enforcement officers, Agent Ryan and his partner excused themselves and went back to their Escalade.

Chance, Alexis, and Black Chief stood quietly next to John's truck. Finally, Black Chief spoke up. "I'll go to tribal court right now and try to get the search warrants for Agent Antone's truck and house. If I can't find a judge on a Friday afternoon, we'll have to wait until Monday morning to get the warrants."

"The sooner the better," said Chance. "But we can wait until Monday if we have to. I don't think Agent Antone is a flight risk, but you know her best, John."

"I don't think she'll flee," answered Black Chief. "I just can't believe she'd be capable of doing such a thing. It's just too crazy and doesn't make any sense. Why would she kill her own partners? And, if she did, why in such a brutal and sadistic way?"

"I agree," said Chance, as he patted John on his shoulder. "Let me and Alexis know when you get the warrants, and we can all go together."

“I’m sorry,” said Alexis, as she touched Black Chief’s arm.

“It’s not your fault, Alexis. In fact, it’s good police work on your part. I just can’t believe my own people would turn on each other like that. It just makes me sick to even think about it,” Black Chief said, shaking his head. “I’ll call you both later this afternoon either way. If I can’t get the warrants on a Friday afternoon, I’ll get them first thing Monday morning. As you’re both fully aware, the judges work pretty much on Indian time, so that means getting the warrants could be a slow process—whenever they’re damn good and ready.”

Stepping away from his detective and the agent, Chance stopped at the Escalade to talk to the feds. “If you don’t mind, gentlemen, before we leave, I’m gonna go to the men’s room and perform my own ‘process of elimination,’ if you know what I mean. Then I’ll be driving back to my office.”

A few minutes later, Chance was back outside and in his Blazer. He waved to his FBI shadows and headed back to his office in Nogales, the federal agents dutifully following him.

Chance stayed in his office catching up on paperwork the rest of the afternoon. Around 1600 hours, he received a call from Agent Black Chief. It appeared the Tribal court judges were indeed on Indian time and had left the office early for the weekend. Agent Black Chief had pleaded to get the warrants today, but the lone judge he got a hold of insisted on meeting Monday morning to hear the details of the case and issue John the needed search warrants. It was just a matter of bad timing; the Tohono O’odham Powwow was being held this weekend, and the sacred ceremonies would take precedence over everything else—including the cold, bloody murders of two of their own people.

Chapter Eight

"Is this one of those extremist cults you read about in the media?" asked Special Agent Ryan, with a look of suspicion and skepticism on his face.

The two feds were standing outside the Empty Brush Sangha with Sheriff Colt. In their crisp black suits, white shirts, red ties, and sunglasses, the agents looked terribly out of place. The people walking by on the dusty sidewalks wore tank tops, flip-flops, straw cowboy hats, and jeans; not a suit was in sight.

Chance had finished up his mound of paperwork for the day at the office and had just showed up for his twice weekly meditation class. "Guys, this is a Buddhist meditation center. *Sangha* is just another word for an assembly or community, where like-minded people go to practice Buddhist meditation together. It's just like any other religion's church. It's a very ancient and peaceful form of philosophy and religion practiced by millions of people in the East and the West. It ain't no cult."

"You'll have to excuse us, Sheriff, but we both come from back East and we don't have these kinds of hippie communes in D.C.," replied Agent Ryan.

"It's not a hippie commune, Agent Ryan. And I'm talking about the Far East, like China, India, Japan, Vietnam, Cambodia—places like that."

"It sounds like an extremist cult to me, like that place in Waco, Texas, back in the nineties," replied Agent Ryan. "Do these people have weapons in there?"

"The only people with weapons will be us, I can guarantee you that," answered Chance. "Come on, guys, really? You've never heard of Zen Buddhism? You can wait in your car for me if you want to, but we encourage visitors to join us for our meditation sessions to learn about the many benefits of studying Buddhism. We're open to everything here."

"Yeah, I'll bet you are," said Agent Ryan. "We'll go in, but we won't be taking our clothes off and getting naked."

"Believe me, the last thing anyone wants to see is you two guys naked. We wear robes. If you don't have a robe, which I know you don't, you can just take off your shoes and socks and sit in your suits."

"Sit?" Agent Ryan inquired.

"Yeah, we sit on pillows in the lotus position."

"Lotus position? What the hell is that?" Agent Ryan asked.

"The lotus position is sittin' cross-legged more or less, with your hands on your knees palms up. Or you can put your hands together in front of you, like praying," Chance explained. "We sit quiet for forty-five minutes and just meditate, which is clearing our minds of all thoughts and just sittin' there in peace. Like the old Buddhist saying goes, 'When you sit, sit. When you stand, stand. Whatever you do, don't wobble.' Get it?"

"Uh, no. Whatever." Agent Ryan shrugged.

Chance tried not to laugh as he walked them inside the meditation center. Agent Ryan and his partner walked stiffly and suspiciously, as if they thought they were about to get waylaid by Ninja warriors.

"Relax, gentlemen," Chance said, trying to reassure the nervous federal agents. "This is supposed to be peaceful and fun. I'll introduce you to my friends. I'm going to the locker room to change into my robe. I'll be right back out. In the meantime, feel free to take a look around."

While Agent Ryan and his partner waited for Chance, they stared suspiciously at the various Buddhist statues, paintings, candles, and altar. The visiting Buddhist teacher walked up to them, introduced himself and politely asked the two federal agents to kindly remove their shoes and socks. They did so, reluctantly, and then were led by the Buddhist monk to their sitting pillows. The monk tried to get the agents to remove their suit jackets, but they both vehemently resisted.

Chance came back out in his satin Zen-style, white full-length kimono robe and met back up with Agent Ryan and his partner, who now appeared ghostly white and were sweating profusely with anxiety and stress.

"You two need to lighten up; you both look like you're about to have a heart attack. Relax, and just let yourself go with the flow," advised Chance.

As the bell softly rang three times to indicate the beginning of the meditation session, Chance pointed toward two pillows in front of him and silently motioned for both federal agents to sit down. Chance sat in the lotus position comfortably on a pillow across from the agents. The agents followed Chance's lead and attempted to sit down cross-legged on their pillows in a lotus position, but neither one of them could stretch their feet above and atop their legs, so they both settled for sitting cross-legged, somewhat American Indian-style. Agent Ryan and his partner attempted to mimic Chance, as he rested his arms and hands palm-up on his knees and closed his eyes to begin to empty his mind of the day's thoughts, stresses, and anxieties.

Chance began to concentrate on slowly breathing in and out, acknowledging and releasing his thoughts with each exhaled breath, and transforming his busy mind to a calm, clear pool of perfectly still water. As he continued deeper into his meditation practice, he temporarily forgot all about the presence of the federal agents. Chance slowly relaxed and unwound as he concentrated on his slowly stilling thoughts. He emptied his mind and began to feel a deep and profound peace, as his breathing and heartbeat slowed considerably in his almost-hypnotic state.

The forty-five minute session seemed to last for only a brief moment, when he heard the bell softly ring once more, indicating the end of another peaceful meditation.

Chance slowly opened his eyes and gently recalled the presence of Agent Ryan and his partner sitting across from him. As all the participants began to rise and tranquilly head for the locker room and eventually toward the exit door to the parking lot, Chance looked at the federal agents with a calm smile on his serene face.

Agent Ryan and his partner began to untangle themselves from their sitting positions, and both of them got up stiffly and with a grimace on their faces. They both were soaking wet from head to toe with perspiration and both had big, round sweat stains under the armpits of their now damp and wrinkled black business suits. They both looked like they had spent the last forty-five minutes being pummeled through an automatic car wash.

"Now, wasn't that refreshing?" asked Chance, with a mischievous grin. "You two guys don't look too good. Should I call 911?"

"You and your Zen Buddhist hippie friends are all crazy, if you think that was refreshing," answered Agent Ryan. "What are you going to do next, go sit and meditate outside on a big rock for another hour?" He gripped the small of his back with his hand and grimaced in pain.

"No, I'm going home to my ranch and spending a quiet evening with my wife."

"I need to go back to the hotel and take some ibuprofen and a long, hot shower," remarked Agent Ryan. "Let's go," he said to his partner, "before I pass out."

"Does that mean you're done following me?" asked Chance. "Have I passed your process of elimination test?"

"At least for tonight," admitted Agent Ryan. "I can't take any more of you today." He threw the Cadillac Escalade keys to his partner and they both limped toward the exit door. "Have a good night, Sheriff Dali Lama," Agent Ryan said sarcastically.

"First, snatch the pebble from my hand, Grasshopper," said Chance with a wide grin.

"Screw you," replied Agent Ryan, as he and his partner stumbled painfully through the door.

When Chance walked out to the parking lot to his truck, dusk was settling in over the western mountains, and the FBI Escalade was nowhere in sight.

Chance sat in his truck watching the full moon slowly rising in the cool, clear desert evening sky. He heard his spirit guide, the long-dead Sheriff White, saying, *I don't trust those damn Federales, They were all crooked and on the take in my day, and they probably still are today, the bastards.*

"I hear you loud and clear, Sheriff White," Chance said aloud to the empty interior of his truck. "I hear you."

Chance woke up on Saturday morning, quickly dressed, and went out to the barn to feed and water the horses. He took Shakespeare with him to the barn, so dog and horses could bid each other a good morning, being the social animals they all were.

Butch and Sundance whinnied with delight when they heard Chance's footsteps and the barn door opening. Both horses stuck their heads out of their stalls and gave Shakespeare a friendly sniff. Shakespeare returned the morning greeting with a wet lick on the lips for each horse.

Chance took his time, talking soothingly to the horses while he gave each one a carrot stick to munch on, and then filled the feed buckets hanging from their stall doors with some oats. He brought in enough hay for the two of them and filled their water buckets with fresh water.

After the horses were done eating breakfast, Chance leisurely brushed down each horse's shiny coat. He enjoyed the companionship of the horses, who nuzzled their noses into his hair, neck, and shoulders, giving him what amounted to an equine hug. Chance then slipped halters on the horses and led them out to the ten-acre grass pasture, past the round training pen, and let the horses loose to get some exercise and grazing—a few hours of horse time in the fresh air.

Chance recalled how he and Sarah bought the small ranch years ago from an old, retiring rancher whose wife had recently passed after a hard-fought battle with cancer. When the wife died, the rancher's heart just wasn't in it any longer, and he sold the livestock and property to them for a song. The day he moved out and Sarah and Chance moved in, the old rancher had smiled politely and tipped his cowboy hat to Sarah and Chance before driving away in his old Ford F-150 pickup truck pulling a two-stall horse trailer packed up with his two favorite horses. He had headed north to Colorado, and neither Chance nor Sarah had ever heard from him again.

Sarah and Chance had always liked the small-town, laid-back feeling of Sonoita, with its population of around eight hundred citizens and its elevation of nearly a mile above sea level, making it significantly cooler than Tucson and many other cities and towns in southern Arizona. It was mostly a ranching community where everyone knew everyone, the people were friendly and tightly knit, and the Code of the West was still alive and well—unlike other more populated areas of the Grand Canyon state.

The name Sonoita came from the Tohono O'odham words "son oidag," best translated as "spring field." Its geography, flora, and fauna made the area look more like Montana than Arizona. Sonoita was situated in a valley of grasslands surrounded by mountains on all sides, making it seem cut off from the rest of the outside world.

This isolation made it a perfect place for Chance to relax and unwind after spending a quarter of a century in law enforcement and eight years in the military as a U.S. Marine scout sniper, after graduating from college. Chance's years of being a Marine and a lawman have taken their toll on him mentally, physically, and psychologically. He had seen and experienced enough war, killing, death, and violence in his time, and he was in dire need of transforming his life in his later years to one filled with an abundance of peace and solitude.

Enjoying that solitude now, Chance sat on the rail of the pasture fence, lost in quiet contemplation with his dog and his horses, drinking in his surroundings with all of his senses until his trance was broken by the ringing of his cell phone. He fished the phone from the front pocket of his jeans, saw Agent's Black Chief's name, and answered on the third ring.

"Sheriff Colt."

"Mornin' Chance," said Black Chief. "Sorry to disturb you, but we have a couple of further developments in the Billy Big Bear and Jim Walking Horse cases that I thought you'd want to be made aware of."

"No problem, John. What have you got?"

"What we've got are two bloody ring fingers appearing to belong to Big Bear and Walking Horse that have arrived today in the U.S. mail addressed to each of the dead men's wives. They both have post office boxes in town off of the rez. As both women were picking up their mail today, each one of them had a nice gift-wrapped box waiting for them. In each box is a man's bloody ring finger, with their gold wedding bands still on the fingers. Seems like the killer or killers are making another bold statement with this move. As you can imagine, both ladies had the bejesus scared out of them, and both brought the fingers to my office. I have the fingers sitting here in front of me on my desk, as we speak. I've been given the finger before, plenty of times, but never like this."

"I'll meet you on the rez at your office in about an hour," said Chance. "We'll bring the fingers to Dr. Patel. He'll be able to determine whether or not they match the two deceased men. I'm sure they will, but he can tell us for sure and take them into evidence. I doubt you've seen any other men running around missing a bloody ring finger in the last couple of days."

"Nope; I can't say that I have," replied Black Chief. "I'll wait for you to get here to my office, just counting the minutes with all of the fingers I have available."

"I'll call Detective Montoya on my way to give her the news and see if she wants to meet us at the county morgue," said Chance. "Keep your fingers crossed that they match the dead men, and I'll be there soon."

"Funny, real funny. I'll be waiting for you so I can get rid of these things ASAP. They're kind of creeping me out, at this point."

"Let's not get too excited and point any fingers just yet," Chance said with a slight smile. "Let's wait until we have them examined."

"You're a very sick man, Sheriff Colt," said Black Chief.

"I can't quite put my finger on it just yet," said Chance, "but I think this may be the break in the case we've been waiting for. At least it points in that direction doesn't it?"

"Stop! Enough!" And Black Chief hung up on Chance.

Chance went back to the house and told his wife about the new evidence. Sarah made a disgusted face, sighed and told Chance to get going.

"I'll be back later," said Chance, as he hurried out the front door and jumped in his truck. He yelled to Shakespeare, as he was pulling away down the driveway, "You stay here with Mom. I don't want you accidentally eating the evidence on the way to the morgue."

Hearing this, Shakespeare stopped running toward the truck and slowly walked back to his usual spot in the shade on the front porch of the house, with his head slung down low and a look of deep disappointment in his soft brown eyes.

Chance telephoned Alexis and Dr. Patel as he drove, explaining the new development and apologizing for ruining their individual days. They all agreed to meet at the county morgue in Nogales. As Chance drove down I-19, he suddenly realized he had lost his tail. He was no longer being followed by FBI Agent Ryan and his partner. The Cadillac Escalade was nowhere in sight.

"Huh," said Chance aloud. "I guess it's true what they say about the FBI. They really don't work weekends. Go figure!"

Chapter Nine

"I've got to hand it to this murderer," Chance said to Agent John Black Chief, as he examined the two boxes on John's desk containing the gift-wrapped bloody fingers. "He or she has got a sense of humor. This could be the start of a new fad like tattoos or body piercings. You cut off dead men's body parts and send 'em to the family, so they can make jewelry out of them. Can I keep Billy Big Bear's finger and make a necklace out of it? Like a rabbit's foot—it could be my good luck charm or keepsake to remember him by."

"You're sick and still not funny, Chance," answered Black Chief. "These two guys were my friends. I don't find anything amusing about any of this body part shit. This was done by someone who is sick, I mean, truly mentally ill."

"I'm sorry, John. I guess I'm just trying to lighten the mood. You're right, though, it's pretty sick. I should probably take Walking Horse's finger instead of Big Bear's. Big Bear's finger is too fat and stubby to make a necklace out of. It would weigh me down too much, and I've got to move light and fast to stay one step ahead of the bad guys," Chance said with a grin, still trying to get a smile out of Black Chief. "Like my grandfather used to say, 'The more you know, the less you need to carry.' Travelling light, quiet, and fast is always your best option."

Black Chief just gave Chance a dirty look as he bagged and tagged the evidence. "Let's drive separate vehicles down to the county morgue in Nogales, so we can go our separate ways after we meet with Dr. Death."

Chance followed Black Chief off of the reservation in his Blazer for the long drive down I-19 to the county morgue. When they arrived, Alexis and the M.E. were already there and waiting for them. Black Chief handed the two evidence bags to Dr. Patel, and all three of them followed the good doctor into his laboratory in a back area of the cold and chemical-smelling morgue.

After taking finger print samples and examining blood from the two ring fingers, Dr. Patel announced his findings.

"Both ring fingers are a match with the deceased," he announced. "One is Billy Big Bear's and the other belongs to Jim Walking Horse. There are no other finger prints or trace evidence on the fingers to indicate the identity of the murderer or murderers. Whoever cut the fingers off and mailed the boxes wore gloves."

"Who would do such a sick thing to the dead men's wives?" mused Black Chief aloud.

"Someone who wanted to make a harsh statement to those wives," said Alexis. "I think Agent Anna Antone was having an affair with both of the husbands and sent the ring fingers of the deceased back to the wives as a message—a sign of these men's infidelity."

"I agree with Alexis," said Chance. "Again, both of these murders were a sign of anger and passion. Never underestimate the wrath of a woman scorned. Now can we get the search warrants for Agent Antone's truck and house, or do we still have to wait until Monday morning for the tribal judges to come back to work from the Powwow?"

"I can try to contact the judges again, but I have a feeling we'll be waiting until Monday," answered Black Chief.

"We could arrest her now," said Alexis, "and hold her and interrogate her until we obtain the physical evidence on Monday."

"What if we're wrong, and it's not Anna Antone?" asked Black Chief.

"What if we're right?" added Chance. "Do we want to take a chance of leaving a killer on the loose until Monday? Who knows, maybe she'll go after the wives next."

"That's just it," said Alexis. "If she's this sick and sadistic, we don't know what she's capable of doing."

Chance and Alexis both looked at Black Chief for an answer.

"All right, we'll arrest her today and hold her over for questioning until we get the search warrants and, hopefully, more physical evidence from her truck or house on Monday," answered Black Chief.

"That will keep us a few steps ahead of Agent Ryan and the FBI," stated Chance, "which is a good thing. We don't want those guys getting to her first and taking credit for this whole investigation, do we?"

"Hell no," said Black Chief. "The victims are my men and my agents. And Anna Antone is my agent. I'm not giving her or this investigation up to the FBI."

"Then let's go get her right now," said Alexis.

"She's scheduled to be working tonight," said Black Chief. "I'll call her and tell her to meet me at my office in an hour. All three of us can be there waiting for her. We just better be right about this," he sighed.

"I know we are," Alexis said with stern conviction in her tone of voice, as she stared confidently into Black Chief's eyes. "You can call it woman's intuition, but she did it."

"Okay," said Black Chief. "Just let me call her in private. I don't want her to know she's being invited into an ambush."

Chance, Alexis, and Dr. Patel left the laboratory and waited in the lobby of the county morgue, giving Black Chief the quiet and privacy he needed to call to Agent Anna Antone. Within one minute, Black Chief met everyone in the lobby and said, "Let's go. She'll be at my office in an hour."

"How did she sound?" asked Chance.

"She sounded normal," said Black Chief.

"They always do," said Alexis.

After they exited the building, Dr. Patel locked the front door of the morgue, then turned and raised a hand in farewell. "Good luck," he said, "and call me if you need anything."

"I need a good psychiatrist. Do you have anyone you could refer me to?" Chance said with a grin.

"I think you're too far gone by now for a psychiatrist to be able to help you," Alexis said drily. "You're too far out of reach to ever make it back to reality."

"Let's go quickly," Black Chief said to Chance and Alexis. "I want all of us to be there at my office before she arrives."

They hurried to their vehicles and sped out of the parking lot, heading to the ICE office on the reservation, in Sells, Arizona. The detective's Dodge Charger and Black Chief's new GMC pickup left Chance's old Chevy Blazer in a cloud of dust. When Chance finally arrived at Black Chief's office building, the Dodge Charger and the GMC truck were the only vehicles parked in the lot. Chance parked his Blazer and walked into the ICE office, where he was immediately blasted with ridicule and sarcasm.

"It's like the race between the turtle and the hare," laughed Alexis.

"You better get a new truck, Sheriff," added Black Chief with a big smile. "Alexis and I have been here for twenty minutes. We averaged a hundred and ten miles per hour. How fast can that old Blazer go?"

"Hey, I got here, didn't I? Me and my Blazer were hauling ass at seventy-five to eighty the whole way. That's pretty damn good for the old girl."

"You must get outrun all the time in that thing by all the old, speeding snow birds," Black Chief barked, as he and Alexis continued to chuckle.

"Guys, she's a classic," said Chance, "a work of art, unlike your two vehicles. She gets me where I need to go in style."

"She's an old hag that needs to be put down, Chance," Black Chief said, clapping the sheriff on the back sympathetically.

"That's what I keep telling him too," said Alexis, "but he's as stubborn as an old mule that loves his old beat-to-hell truck. One of these days that truck is going to get you killed, Sheriff."

"Hey, nobody lives forever," said Chance. "Now can we quit the joking and get down to business before Antone gets here? I want to make the arrest. After all, the murders occurred in my county."

"Sorry, but you're on tribal land now," Black Chief reminded him, "So that makes this my arrest and my prisoner. You have no authority on my reservation, remember? Tribal sovereignty takes precedence here. If you're nice to me, I may let you and Alexis interview her. But when she walks in, she's mine."

They all sat in Black Chief's office and waited patiently. Within minutes, a Shadow Wolf vehicle drove up and parked in the lot next to the other three vehicles. Shadow Wolf Agent Anna Antone jumped out and walked inside the building. She stopped at Black Chief's office door and looked at all three law enforcement officers waiting for her.

"What is this—a surprise party?" she exclaimed. "It's not even close to my birthday." She stepped inside her boss's office with a surprised smile on her face.

Black Chief went to Anna Antone and grasped her right arm. "Agent Anna Antone, you're under arrest for the murders of Jim Walking Horse and Billy Big Bear."

The smile disappeared from Anna's face as Black Chief handcuffed her, removed her duty weapon from her possession, and placed the firearm on his desk. He then performed a quick but thorough body search for any other weapons, emptied her pocket contents out onto his desk, and finally led her briskly and with authority to one of the four holding cells located in the rear of the building.

"You've got to be kidding me," Anna said, as she looked out of the cell at her boss for some kind of an explanation. Black Chief slammed the cell door closed, ensured that it was secure, and read Anna's Miranda rights to her. Then he walked straight back into his office without speaking another word to her. He shut his office door behind him, sat at his desk, and faced Chance and Alexis.

"Okay, what's the game plan for the interrogation?"

"I think Alexis has the best shot at breaking her," said Chance. "She's more likely to confess to another woman than a man. Let's play good cop—Alexis—and bad cop—me."

"Chance, she's not stupid," said Black Horse. "She's a federal agent. She's not going to fall for that old routine."

"Well, we've got nothin' but time on our hands till we get those search warrants on Monday, so we have lots of time to try different interrogation techniques. Let me start off, and I'll warm her up for you, Alexis."

Black Chief shrugged. "You can try."

He went back to the holding cell and walked Anna down to one of the interview rooms. Like most such facilities, it had a one-way mirror on one wall so they could look in at her but she couldn't see out at them. It also had a small table, three wooden chairs, and a recording device.

Chance stepped into the interview room and closed the door behind him. He went to the table where Anna sat silently and sat down next to her. Slowly and deliberately he removed his brown felt cowboy hat and set it on the table, positioning it just so—upside down, or brim-side up. He smiled politely at Anna and began his oft-rehearsed introduction.

"Anna, my name is Sheriff Chance Colt. I've been the sheriff of Santa Cruz County for the past twenty-five years." He gestured at his cowboy hat. "Do you know why a man always sets his cowboy hat brim up when he takes it off?"

"No." Anna stared at the hat, like she was waiting for a magic rabbit to hop out.

"It's so the luck don't run out. That's what my grandfather always used to say, anyway. I'm not one to test the fates, so I always place my hat brim up. And you know what, Anna? For twenty-five years my luck ain't run out. Go figure, huh?"

"I'm not sure why you're telling me this."

"Well, Anna, I'm here to tell you that yours has." Chance stopped talking and looked straight into Anna's brown eyes.

"My what has—what?" asked Anna.

"Your luck has run out. Do you understand your Miranda rights, as they were explained to you by Agent Black Chief?"

Anna let out a short laugh and glared straight back into Chance's green eyes with a look of steadfast determination. She set her jaw hard and pushed it out toward him. "Lawyer."

"What?" asked Chance.

"Lawyer," stated Anna, with a steely-eyed stare. "I've got nothing to say to you, sheriff. I want to speak with my lawyer."

Chapter Ten

"I got her all loosened up for you, Alexis. This will be a piece of cake for you," Chance announced, as he strolled back into Black Chief's office with a confident gate and a twinkle in his eye. "I think she'll break within fifteen minutes of you talking to her." He smiled as he placed his cowboy hat back on his head.

"Oh, don't tell me—did you use the old 'cowboy hat brim up and your luck has just run out routine'?" asked Alexis.

"I sure did," answered Chance. "It worked like a charm. She'll be crying like a baby and confessing to you within minutes. Go get her, Tiger. She's all yours."

Alexis gave Chance a suspicious look as she stood to leave the room. "You weren't even in there with her five minutes."

"We professional interrogators work fast," Chance quipped. "I've got her on the ropes for you. You just need to go in for the knockout."

Alexis left Black Chief's office for the interrogation room. Black Chief leaned back in his chair, his hands behind his head. "Is she really about to break?"

"Hell no. She only said one word to me, and that was 'lawyer.' She's gonna be a tough nut to crack."

"I told you, she's a sharp woman, Chance. She's not going to fall for any cheap cop tricks."

"Then, it'll make Monday all the more fun, when we get the warrants and the physical evidence we need against her."

"I hope you're right," said Black Chief. "Otherwise, Anna Antone is never gonna forgive me."

Within five minutes Alexis stormed back into Black Chief's office and slammed the door shut, her face beet red. "You're full of shit, Sheriff Colt!" she yelled, pointing a finger at Chance's face. "All she would say is 'lawyer,' and then she clammed up. She's in there right now laughing at both of us."

"Really? When I left the room, she was about ready to break. It must be you, Alexis." Chance smiled a devilish smile. "I had her on the ropes."

"Bull shit!" Alexis sat down in a chair with a furious look on her face.

"Well, maybe I misjudged her a little bit," Chance said. "I'm just kidding with you, Alexis. Anna Antone is one tough cookie. That's all she would say to me, too."

"I'm not even going to try with her, then," said Black Chief. "She already hates me. I'll just put her back in the holding cell while you two geniuses come up with a Plan B."

Black Chief left the office and quickly returned after escorting Anna Antone back to her holding cell. He walked back into his office and sat back down behind his desk. "Well?"

"Plan B is we let her just sit and stew until we get the search warrants on Monday," Chance offered up.

"Great plan," said Black Chief. "You're a regular Dick Tracy, Sheriff."

"It's Saturday night. Let's all go home and get some sleep. Maybe we can think of a better plan in the morning. In the meantime, we let our suspect sit and stew. Speaking of stew, I'm starving. You guys want to stop for dinner somewhere before we call it a night?"

"Not me," said Alexis. "I'm going home to bed."

"Me too," added Black Chief. "Let's touch base with each other in the morning. And tomorrow I'll try to get in touch with one of the tribal judges one more time, if I can find one who's not at the Powwow."

Chance drove home, had dinner with Sarah and William Shakespeare, and then fell sound asleep in his rocking chair while reading *Zen Flesh, Zen Bones,* next to the slowly burning fire of mesquite wood in his fireplace. Sarah and Shakespeare both abandoned him and went up to bed to sleep more comfortably in the king-sized bed in the master bedroom.

Chance's cell phone woke him, once again, before he'd gotten a full night's sleep. He checked the time: it was just after 0400 hours on Sunday morning, as he was having his usual dreams involving the late Sheriff White.

"This is Sheriff Colt," he said.

"Deputy Graves here. Sorry to wake you, Sheriff."

"Do I have to get a restraining order against you?" Chance said. "You really need to leave me alone in the middle of the night. Are you the only deputy working the graveyard shift nowadays?" There was dead silence on the other end of the line. "I'm joking with you, Deputy. What do you have?"

"Oh. Okay. What we have appears to be an aggravated sexual assault on a young lady, a teenager fifteen years of age, by the name of Esperanza Gonzales."

"She was raped?"

"That's what she's claiming, sir."

"Where are you at?"

"I'm at Holy Cross Hospital in Rio Rico in the waiting room with the victim's mother and father. The parents and the hospital called our department to report the rape, and I just happened to be working District One tonight, so I got the call."

"Gotcha. I'll meet you at the hospital and call Detective Montoya to meet the both of us, as well. I'll be there within the hour."

"Thanks, Sheriff. I'll wait for you, along with the parents."

Chance hung up the phone and immediately dialed his detective's cell phone.

"Detective Montoya," Alexis answered sleepily.

"Good morning, Alexis. This is Chance. Sorry to wake you so early, but we have another case I need your help on."

"Not another dead Indian with a missing ring finger, I hope?"

"No, this one is a possible sexual assault of a fifteen-year-old girl in Rio Rico. I know we're busy with the Shadow Wolf murders, but I think you would be the best choice for this case also. It sounds like it may be a sensitive one that will require a woman's involvement and a woman's touch."

"Where do I need to meet you?" asked Alexis.

"At Holy Cross Hospital in Rio Rico. The victim is there, and Deputy Graves is with her mom and dad in the waiting room now."

"Graves, again? Is he the only deputy we have working on graveyard shift at this point? Why do we always get Graves?"

"It's just the luck of the draw. He's working District One tonight. Can you meet me at the hospital in an hour?"

"I'll be there," answered Alexis. "See you soon."

Chance hung up the phone and got up from the rocking chair holding the small of his back and then massaging his right knee. "You're too old to sleep in a rocking chair," he said to himself. He limped off to the bathroom to take some ibuprofen, wash his face, and clean up as quickly as he could. He put on a fresh t-shirt and long-sleeved button-down shirt, along with a new pair of jeans. On his way out of the house, he literally ran into Shakespeare, who had gotten out of bed to see what all the commotion was about. Chance put on his boots and hat and let Shakespeare out to take care of business.

"Sorry, buddy. You have to stay here with Mom again. They don't allow dogs in the hospital, and I may be quite a while," Chance explained to Shakespeare as he let him back into the house. Shakespeare looked sleepy-eyed at Chance, as if he were relieved he didn't have to go to work. The dog released a big yawn and slowly headed back upstairs to the king-sized bed to get some more shut-eye with Sarah.

"Good dog," said Chance. "I'll be back later." He shut and locked the front door of the house and hurried to his truck. He jumped in the Blazer, started her up, and headed for the town of Rio Rico.

When he arrived at the hospital, Alexis was already there and was speaking quietly with Deputy Graves just outside the door of the girl's private room. Chance joined in on their conversation.

"What have we got so far?"

"The victim, Esperanza Gonzales, who lives in Rio Rico with her mom and dad, was at a party with two of her female high school friends at a private residence at—" Alexis flipped through her notes, "—506 Camino Hombre De Oro in Rio Rico. According to the victim's two girlfriends, Esperanza was last seen talking with a young, white male at the party, approximately twenty to twenty-two years of age, short blond hair, a blond goatee, and approximately six feet tall and two hundred pounds wearing a red U of A t-shirt and jeans."

"U of A? Figures," said Graves, who had attended ASU if Chance remembered correctly.

"Whatever, Graves," Alexis said. "Anyway, her friends told her parents they found Esperanza about an hour later, naked and unconscious on the bathroom floor in the master bathroom of the house. When Esperanza woke up, her friends left the party and immediately drove her to her mom and dad's house."

"Got info on them?" Chance asked.

"Of course. Her parents gave me the names of her two girlfriends and their contact information so we can follow up with them and get statements later today."

Chance glanced over at the parents. He could see them through the open door, standing by their daughter's bedside. The mother looked like she'd been crying.

"The parents said Esperanza admitted to drinking a few beers and talking to the male suspect, who eventually led her to the master bathroom," Alexis went on. "She told her parents the suspect started kissing and fondling her—and then she blacked out. She doesn't remember anything after that until her girlfriends found her naked on the bathroom floor, woke her up, and drove her home. The parents then brought her straight to the E.R."

"What did the doctors find?" Chance asked.

"Initial testing by the hospital staff with a rape kit indicates she was vaginally penetrated, her hymen was broken, and there is evidence of blood, semen, and gunpowder residue present, both in her vagina and in her underwear. She has a contusion on her skull, which means she'll be kept overnight for observation. I took written statements from the hospital staff, but I haven't had time to interview Esperanza or the parents in-depth. I'll get written statements from all of them."

"Gunpowder residue in her vagina?" Chance scratched his head under his hat. "Let's make sure we get a copy of all the hospital records and test results on this gal. Graves, can you visit the nurse's station, talk to the doctor, and get copies of all their records and testing up till now?"

"You got it, Sheriff." Graves headed for the nurse's station.

"Alexis, how about I interview and obtain statements from both parents while you interview the victim. I know I don't have to tell you this, but let's take it real easy and slow with the victim, due to her age and the trauma she's been through, and let's be extremely thorough. I want to get this right the first time and take the suspect into custody as quickly as possible, if he can be positively identified."

"I'll go interview Esperanza right now," Alexis said. "I'll meet up with you and Graves when we're all done here. Then I want to contact Esperanza's two girlfriends and interview them ASAP."

"We'll get statements from the two girlfriends and then we'll hit the house and home owner at 506 Camino Hombre De Oro," Chance said. "If he or she doesn't cooperate and grant us permission to enter and search the premises, we'll go obtain a search warrant from the court in Nogales. Good luck with the girl."

Alexis nodded and headed for the girl's hospital room with a look of determination on her face and fire in her eyes.

Chance arranged to meet with the parents in the waiting room. They appeared to be disillusioned, saddened, and in shock. He introduced himself and launched into the interview, as gently as he could.

"I want to say, first off, how sorry I am about this happening to your daughter. However, I can assure you that me and my department will do anything and everything possible to ensure the safety and proper care of your daughter and complete our investigation of this terrible crime to the best of our abilities and bring the suspect into custody as soon as is possible, so he can be held responsible to answer and pay for his heinous acts committed against your daughter."

The parents thanked Chance for his kind words. They both looked extremely tired, afraid, and worried for the welfare of their daughter, and the expressions on their faces pulled hard at Chance's heartstrings.

"Do you mind if I ask you both a few questions separately?" Chance asked. "I just want to get as much background information as we can, so we can figure out what happened to Esperanza and arrest her assailant before he hurts anyone else. Do you mind taking a walk outside with me first, Mr. Gonzales? I can talk with you, and, then with your wife for a few minutes."

"Of course," answered Mr. Gonzales, "and please call me Hector."

The two men walked outside together and sat on a park bench. Chance wanted to make Hector Gonzales feel at ease so he could obtain as much information as possible and also get a good read on the father's character and personality and what kind of a parent he was. These days, Chance never took it for granted that he was talking to an innocent witness, so he always attempted to form a professional opinion—or what Chance called his cop sense—on what kind of person he was dealing with.

Immediately after they started talking, Chance's cop sense told him that Hector Gonzales was a straight arrow and a good parent who felt genuine concern for his daughter's welfare. Hector's daughter had told her parents that she was going to a high school classmate's party at a friend's house. When Esperanza's friends brought her home from the party, they had said it was a typical high school party at a friend's house. However, sometime during the evening, four or five male University of Arizona students had shown up at the residence.

In response to Chance's query, Mr. Gonzales stated he wasn't aware of Esperanza being friends with or even knowing any college-age boys. Chance shared the suspect's description as given by Esperanza's two friends. Mr. Gonzales stated he wasn't aware of anyone he or his daughter knew who would fit that description.

Chance thanked Mr. Gonzales for answering his questions and reassured him he would do everything in his power to find and arrest Esperanza's attacker. The two men walked back into the hospital to the waiting room and Mrs. Gonzales. Chance handed Mr. Gonzales his business card with both his office and cell phone numbers and assured him he could be reached at any time, day or night, if he could be of service to the Gonzales family.

Outside with Mrs. Gonzales, the sheriff asked her the same questions he had asked her husband. Chance's cop sense immediately picked up on the mother's sincerity and the frightened verbal and non-verbal characteristics and mannerisms she clearly displayed. After she gave him similar answers to those her husband had given, he gave her the same reassurances about doing everything in their power to find and arrest Esperanza's attacker as quickly as possible. He then escorted Mrs. Gonzales back inside the hospital to be with her husband.

Chance waited outside Esperanza's room for Alexis to conclude her interview with the victim. After approximately an hour, Alexis stepped out, and they went to speak with the parents so Alexis could update them on what she had learned from Esperanza. After giving a brief summary to the parents, Alexis and Chance went to the hospital cafeteria to update each other and compare notes on the case developments thus far.

"Just to let you know straight off," Alexis began, "I just flat out lied my ass off to the parents."

"What do you mean?" Chance asked, as they both grabbed a cup of coffee and sat down at a table in the back of the cafeteria, so they could be alone and talk more privately.

"I lied about what their daughter told me about the attack. I didn't think they'd be ready to hear the gory details yet. It's too much."

"Well, tell me," said Chance.

"Esperanza didn't black out. She was awake through the whole ordeal until her assailant hit her over the head with his pistol, which briefly knocked her unconscious. Her girlfriends found her on the bathroom floor and were able to wake her up. She's got a big, bloody knot on the top of her head. I think you should hear Esperanza's story straight from her. I want to see if she tells it the same way again to you, so we know it's true and accurate. If her story is accurate, this SOB, her assailant, is one sick guy who needs to die."

"Let's go back to her room, and I'll talk to her this time," Chance said. "But do you think she'll feel safe and comfortable talking to a man about what happened to her?"

"Yeah, I think she'll be okay talking to you, just go easy and be sensitive with her, like you advised me. She's got to tell you this story herself. I'm too shocked and pissed off right now to repeat what she told me," said Alexis, her own eyes tearing up. "Besides, like I said, I want to hear her tell it again to get an idea of how accurate and true it is "If it's true, I'm going to kill this SOB when we find him."

Alexis and Chance finished their coffee and walked back to the victim's room. Chance asked the parents for permission to chat with their daughter privately; they seemed reluctant but returned to the waiting room. The sheriff and his detective entered the girl's semi-darkened hospital room and closed the door behind them.

Alexis stepped to the bedside, where the girl appeared to be sleeping, her face turned away. She touched the teen's arm. "Esperanza? It's me, Alexis. I brought a friend of mine with me this time to talk with you. This is Sheriff Chance Colt, the sheriff of Santa Cruz County."

"Hi, Esperanza." Chance saw her turn toward them, her eyes opening and a questioning look appearing on her face. She looked younger than fifteen, with her heart-shaped face, wide eyes, and long, black hair.

He removed his cowboy hat and sat in the chair at the side of her hospital bed. He wanted to be positioned where he could look straight into her eyes, and where she could clearly see his face as well. "I'm very sorry for what's happened to you," he said in his gentlest tone, "and I want you to know that Alexis and I are going to find the man who hurt you. I just need you to tell me everything you can remember, so we can make sure you get all the care you need and we can find the guy who hurt you before he gets the chance to hurt anyone else. Do you think you can do that for me, Esperanza?"

"Yes, Sheriff." Esperanza swallowed hard and looked up at Chance with big, brown, innocent eyes, as wide as coffee cup saucers.

"Please, call me Chance," the sheriff said softly as his heart began to slowly break. "I'm your friend, and I'm here to help you and keep you safe. That guy will never hurt you again, Chance's Honor," he said, as he held up his right hand to her like a pledge.

"Okay, Chance," said the petite, fragile-looking teen. "Where do you want me to start?"

"At the very beginning, so I make sure I understand everything exactly as it happened, okay?"

"Has anyone ever told you that Chance is kind of a funny name?" Esperanza said with a trusting smile.

"Why, yes, they have," Chance answered with a broad grin. This fifteen-year-old was proving more resilient and brave than he had expected. "I guess it kind of describes me and what I do. I give nice people like you a second chance with their lives, so to speak."

"I like that," said Esperanza. "That makes sense, and it makes me feel a little better." She took a deep breath, and then she reached out and held onto Chance's right hand as she began to speak. "My two girlfriends, Maria and Melinda—we go to high school together. We heard about a friend's party that he was having at his house, so we decided to go to it."

"What is your friend's name that had the party?" asked Chance. He wasn't taking notes—it would be too distracting to the girl—but Alexis was recording the conversation.

"His name is Ricardo Rodriguez. He's a sophomore at our school with us."

"Was the party held at Ricardo's house or his parent's house?"

"The party was at Ricardo's parent's house. He lives there with his family."

"Were Ricardo's parents' home during the party?"

"I don't think so. I didn't see them," answered Esperanza.

"Have you ever met Ricardo's parents before?"

"No, I never met his parents. I just know Ricardo from school."

"Okay, go ahead and tell me what happened when you got to the party," continued Chance.

"Well, Melinda drove the three of us, because she's sixteen and she has her driver's license and an old car that her dad bought for her. We got to the party about 8:30, and there were already thirty or forty kids there."

"Were they all high school kids? I mean, kids that you knew?"

"Most of them, yeah, but there were also a few older guys that said they go to college at the University of Arizona in Tucson," she continued.

"Did you know the college guys, or have you ever seen them before?"

"No, I didn't know any of them before tonight. I just met them and saw them for the first time tonight at the party."

"And how many college guys were there?"

"I saw about six or seven older guys altogether, but I've never seen them before. I didn't meet all of them. I only talked to the one."

"The one college guy that you talked to, what was his name?"

"He told me his name was Steven. I don't remember his last name. I don't know if he ever told me. Wait, he did tell me his last name. He said his name was Steven Styles. I remember now because I thought it was a cool name, kind of like a movie star's name."

"Did he spell it for you? Like was it S-T-I-L-E-S or S-T-Y-L-E-S?"

"I don't know. I didn't ask him to spell it. I just thought it was a cool name."

"What did he look like? Can you describe him as best as you can for me?"

"Yeah, when I first met him I thought he was hot. He was probably about twenty to twenty-two years old, about six feet tall, and I'd say he weighed around two hundred pounds. He was a pretty big guy. He had short blond hair, like a crew cut, like he was a jock or played sports. He had a blond goatee and mustache and beautiful blue eyes. Like I said, he was very good-looking, like a movie star or an athlete."

"Did he have any distinguishing marks, like freckles, moles, scars, or tattoos?"

"Not on his face that I can remember. Like I said, he looked like a movie star, kind of like a young Brad Pitt, with short blond hair and dreamy blue eyes. When he took off his shirt in the bathroom, I did notice a scar on his abs."

"Was the scar on his right side or his left side of his abdomen, and how long was it?"

"I'm pretty sure it was lower down on his right side and probably about six inches long."

"Did it look like a scar he would have gotten from having some kind of surgery, or was it more like an uneven cut, like he may have gotten in a knife fight?"

"It looked straight and I remember there were stitch marks, like it was sewn up by a doctor."

"And it was definitely on his lower right side of his abdomen?"

"Yeah, I'm pretty positive."

"Good, Esperanza. Now tell me how you ended up in the bathroom with him. And don't be afraid that I'll judge you, because you didn't do anything wrong. Not a thing. You're the victim here."

"Well, like I said, he was really good looking, and he came up and started talking to me and my friends. He offered me a beer in a red plastic cup from a keg of beer they had sitting on top of the bar in the living room. So I took the beer and started to drink it kind of slow while he talked to me."

"Was he drinking beer too?"

"Yeah, he had a plastic cup full of beer like the one he gave me. Eventually he seemed to be talking more to me than to Maria and Melinda, so they walked away to talk to other people."

"Was Steven Styles alone or did he come to the party with others?"

"From the first time I saw him by the beer keg and the bar, he was alone. I never saw him talk to or with anyone else."

"What did you and Steven talk about?"

"Well, he kept telling me how pretty I was. He said I was the most beautiful girl at the party. He talked a little about how he was going to school at the U of A, but mostly he kept talking about me and how pretty he thought I was. The whole time we talked, he kept refilling my cup and his cup with more beer. Eventually, I told him I was feeling a little dizzy and light-headed and needed to pee from drinking all of the beer. He said he would show me where the bathroom was at so I could go, and he led me upstairs to the second floor of the house."

"Were there any other people upstairs on the second floor? Anyone that might have seen you two up there?"

"No, it was dark and quiet, so I don't think anyone else was upstairs. He took my hand and led me down the hallway to what looked like a master bedroom because it was big, like it was Ricardo's parents' bedroom. We walked through the dark bedroom, and he led me into the master bathroom, which was also big, and he turned on the lights so I could see where I was going. I felt kind of awkward peeing in front of him, but I had to go really bad. He told me he would turn around and face the door while I went to the bathroom."

She paused, and Chance saw tears forming in her eyes.

"I know this is hard, Esperanza, but I need you to tell me the rest. You're doing great!"

"When he turned around, I pulled down my jeans and panties and sat on the toilet to pee. I noticed at that point he locked the door, and then he turned around and helped me up from the toilet when I was finished. I pulled up my pants and washed my hands in the sink, and that's when he came up real close behind me. I turned around and he kissed me on the lips. He kept kissing me and touching me with his hands and telling me how pretty I was."

Esperanza stopped talking at this point. She took her hand away from Chance's, looked down and away from him, and began to weep and hug herself. Until this point, she had looked him straight in the eye the whole time as she talked. Now, however, she looked straight down at her hospital bed blanket and sheets, as if she were ashamed. She pulled the blanket and sheets up close, covering herself all the way up to her neck.

Chance patted her shoulder, and she flinched. "I'm sorry," he said. "I can only imagine how difficult this is for you to talk about, especially to a stranger and a man. I'm here to help, and like I said, you didn't do anything wrong. The only way we can bring this criminal to justice is for you to tell me everything that happened. Can you do that—please?"

Esperanza wiped the tears from her eyes and nodded. She took another deep breath and continued her story in stark detail. "He kept touching me and kissing me and telling me how beautiful I was. I was very scared at this point, but I also liked it. He was touching me so softly and tenderly that I thought he really cared for me, and I didn't want him to stop, so I let him keep going."

She was talking through her tears now, her breath catching. "He—he took off his t-shirt and, like I said, he was beautiful. I let him lift up my shirt and take it off, and he pulled me closer to him and kissed me more. His body felt hot to the touch, and we were both sweating. I guess I just let him go, and he kept undressing me while he was kissing and caressing me and holding me tightly to him. He took off my bra, my jeans, and my panties, and before I realized what was happening, I was completely naked. I should have been embarrassed, but I was kind of drunk, and it felt so warm and good, I let him keep doing it.

"He took off his jeans and boxer shorts and continued to caress, fondle, and kiss me all over, and I let him, because, again, it felt warm and good. His body felt so hot and hard against mine, and his thing—his, um, penis—was big and hard. When he took off his jeans, that's when I noticed the gun clipped to his belt."

"What did the gun look like?"

"It was a pistol; a black pistol."

"Did it have a cylinder, like an old-fashioned revolver, like from a cowboy movie?" Chance asked. "Or did it look like the modern guns you see today in the movies or on television that would be called a semi-automatic pistol?"

"It looked like the guns you see in movies and on TV today. It wasn't like an old-fashioned cowboy gun."

"What happened next?"

"Well, when I saw the gun, that's when I really got scared. I told him that he was scaring me and that I wanted to put my clothes back on, leave, and go back downstairs with my friends. That's when his attitude changed and he was no longer nice and started to get mean. He pointed the gun at the side of my head, actually pushing the gun barrel against my ear and the side of my head. He told me to do what he said or he would kill me."

"What were his exact words when he threatened you?"

"I know exactly what he said: 'If you don't do what I say, I'll kill you, bitch.' Then he made me sit down on the toilet and continued to hold the gun to the side of my head to the point where it hurt. He told me to take a hold of his thing—his penis, and he forced me to put it in my mouth. He then made me suck it, you know, what do you call it, 'give him head.' I did it because I was scared he was really going to shoot me if I didn't. Within a couple of minutes he came, ejaculated or whatever you call it, in my mouth. I was gagging at this point and spit it all out of my mouth and onto the bathroom floor."

"That must have been very scary for you," Chance said. He glanced at Alexis, who had a look of pure fury on her face. Chance wished he had his hands on the perp's neck right about then. He'd teach him a thing or two about the right way to treat little girls.

"Yeah, I just sat there shaking and crying, but he was laughing at me. He stayed standing in front of me with the gun still pointed at my head. I think that's when I noticed the scar on his abs, the one I told you about earlier. He kept laughing and pushing the gun hard against the side of my head and kept telling me to be quiet and shut up. Then he told me to get down on the floor and lay on my back and spread my legs open. The tile floor was cold and I was shaking from the cold and fear, but I lay on the floor like he told me to do because he was still pointing the gun at my face.

"When I lay on my back on the floor, he knelt down in front of me and pushed my legs apart with the barrel of the gun. Then he started pushing and then forcefully shoving the barrel of the gun in and out of my—my—you know. He shoved the gun in and out so hard that it started to hurt, and I started to bleed down there between my legs. I kept trying to push my legs together, but he kept pulling them apart. Then he lay down on top of me with all his weight. I could hardly breathe from having all of his weight on top of me and from crying. He put his gun up to the side of my head again and told me to shut up and be quiet or he would kill me."

"He put his thing inside me, in my—you know, and I guess I just gave up and stopped fighting him. I just closed my eyes, I cried, and I waited for it to be over. He stayed there, on top of me, moving around and grunting for a few minutes, and then he kind of collapsed.

"When it was finally over, he stood above me while he got dressed, putting his underwear, his jeans and his t-shirt back on, while still pointing the gun at me and telling me over and over again to be quiet and shut up. I tried to keep quiet, but I was shaking and—and crying so hard I almost couldn't breathe. The last thing I remember was that he told me I was beautiful again and that he was going to make me his girlfriend. He said he would be my only boyfriend. He told me I was now his and no other man could ever touch me but him. He told me he loved me.

"The last thing I remember seeing was him holding the gun up over his head and swinging it down hard at my head. I closed my eyes and I think it knocked me unconscious, because when I woke up, he was gone and Maria and Melinda were the only ones with me in the bathroom. I told them I wanted to go home, and they helped me get dressed. Then we ran out of the house to Melinda's car, and we cried all the way home to my parent's house."

"Melinda and Maria helped me walk inside my house, and they both yelled for my mom and dad. My parents were asleep but they got out of bed and they drove me to the hospital. And here I am." Esperanza wiped the tears from her eyes and looked up once again into Chance's eyes, as if she were asking, *What now?* He took her small, brown hand in his and told her she was safe now, and he would never let that man hurt her ever again.

Esperanza, Alexis, and Chance sat quietly together without talking for a few minutes. Chance knew the girl's parents must be anxious to see her. Just about the time he was heading out to get them, he saw that Esperanza was quietly and peacefully sleeping. He carefully let go of her hand and placed it by her side. Watching her sleep, he thought again that she didn't even look fifteen years old. She looked like a small, delicate child, and his eyes began to fill with tears. He let them flow until there were no more, dabbing at them with his sleeve. When they dried up, a familiar and well-recognized feeling came back to him, deep in his chest, like an old friend: it was silent and determined anger, even rage.

As he had done so many times before in his life, first as a young U.S. Marine scout sniper and later as an Arizona lawman, he allowed the Shadow Man to emerge from deep inside himself, once again. He would willingly release the Shadow Man and let the hunter, predator, and warrior come out from dormancy to seek justice, retribution, and revenge.

The Shadow Man was that part of him he disliked the most. He had spent a lifetime trying to keep it hidden from others in the deep recesses of his soul and to put it away for good, letting it lie dormant and silent, with the hope that this part of him would slowly fade away and die a proud and noble death. However, it was not to be. The Shadow Man was as much a part of Chance and his life as the rest of him was: the good, the bad, the ugly. It seemed Chance Colt could never fully escape from the Shadow Man deep within. It was a part of his destiny and a part of why he was who he was.

As William Shakespeare (the playwright, not the pup) once explained, "All the world's a stage, and each of us must play a part." Chance's part to play was peaceful warrior and defender of all mankind. Unfortunately, sometimes, that job required him to play judge, jury, and executioner.

Chapter Eleven

Some American Indians believe that inside each individual human being lies a Shadow Man. The Shadow Man only comes out in the worst of circumstances: in times of fear, in times of desperation, and in times of necessity in order to defend ourselves or others from worldly danger and harm. It is the "dark side" of man, but a side of him that is necessary for survival and to defend and deliver oneself and others from the evils that are ever-present in this world.

Once the Shadow Man has performed his necessary duty, we must learn to put him back deep inside ourselves once more, until the time comes when he is needed again. Chance hoped and prayed that the day finally would come on this earth when human beings no longer had a need or use for the Shadow Man. Then he could, once and for all, slowly fade away into dust. However, as long as there was evil present in this world, there would always be a need for the Shadow Man to remain in waiting for the time he would be forced to come out, once again, to seek and deliver truth, justice, revenge, and final victory of good over evil.

After leaving Esperanza at the hospital with her parents and a twenty-four hour guard posted just outside her hospital room door, Chance and Alexis drove separate vehicles to the house where the rape had occurred, 506 Camino Hombre De Oro in Rio Rico, the house where Ricardo Rodriguez lived. They arrived at the house at approximately 0800 hours on Sunday morning.

Chance rang the doorbell and knocked firmly and loudly on the front door of the house for several minutes before a young Hispanic male finally opened the door. Chance had positioned himself to the right of the front door and Alexis stood to the left for their own self-protection. Both Chance and Alexis were seasoned and experienced law enforcement officers who understood the risks of the job and always took precautions in an unknown and potentially volatile situation. A cop who stands in front of a door he knocks on is liable to get himself shot through the closed door by a would-be assailant.

The teen stood in the doorway dressed only in a pair of jeans, with no shirt, shoes, or socks, Chance grabbed him by his left arm, pulled him fully out of the house, and threw him face down on the ground before searching him for weapons. Finding none, Chance apologized for the rough treatment as he helped the boy to his feet. Chance explained to the shocked and still half-asleep young man that searching him was necessary for the sheriff's and Detective Montoya's personal safety.

Chance asked the teen his name and if anyone else was presently inside the house. The stunned young man identified himself as Ricardo Rodriguez and stated there was no one else at home at the moment. Ricardo explained that he lived there with his parents, who were presently out of town visiting relatives in Nogales.

Sheriff Colt and Detective Montoya asked the young man a series of questions pertaining to the party that was held on the premises the previous night. Ricardo was cooperative in answering all of their questions. Chance then asked Ricardo's permission to search the house without a warrant.

Ricardo hesitated to allow the search, so Chance informed him that Esperanza Gonzales had been sexually abused in his house during the party. Ricardo looked stunned, stated he was a friend of Esperanza's from school, and immediately gave Sheriff Colt and Detective Montoya permission to search the entire home.

Chance asked Ricardo what time the party had ended and when the last guests had departed. Ricardo answered that all of his guests had left the house by approximately 3 a.m. Chance then asked if Ricardo had cleaned the place up yet after the party, and Ricardo said that he hadn't cleaned anything because he was tired. After the last guest left, he had locked the front door and gone up to his bedroom to sleep. He said he slept until the sheriff's knock on the door woke him up.

Ricardo, Chance, and Alexis entered the house and began by walking through the first floor, which contained a living room or great room, a kitchen, a dining room, and a guest bathroom. Chance observed empty red plastic cups strewn about each room, along with an empty beer keg sitting on top of the bar in the living room. Remnants and debris from the party were everywhere, and the whole downstairs of the house looked like a disheveled war zone.

Ricardo definitely had no time to clean up before going to sleep, Chance thought to himself, *which means that the scene of the crime in the master bathroom most likely is undisturbed as well.*

Chance asked Ricardo to lead him and his detective upstairs to the second level of the home. On the second floor they found a long hallway, three bedrooms, and a hall bathroom that appeared neat, clean, orderly, and undisturbed, with the exception of Ricardo's bed, which was unmade and looked recently slept in.

Sheriff Colt and Detective Montoya walked through all of the rooms, saving the master bedroom for last. The master bedroom also looked undisturbed. However, when they entered the master bathroom, the alleged crime scene, it was a mess.

Ricardo's eyes opened wide, as he peered through the door into his parent's master bathroom. None of them actually set foot into the bathroom; they all just studied the scene from the doorway. The bathroom looked like a crime scene, with blood stains and what appeared to be dried semen on the brown ceramic tile floor, blood spattered along the sink and countertop, and used and bloody yellow bath towels and two empty red plastic beer cups thrown on the floor.

Chance turned to Ricardo, who was now white as a ghost, and asked if he could have his permission to order a crime scene investigation and have an evidence technician come out to go over and through the bathroom to collect any and all physical evidence. Ricardo immediately consented, and went and sat down on his parents' bed, holding his head in his hands and closing his eyes in disbelief.

Chance called for an evidence technician to be dispatched to the premises ASAP and gave the home address to the county dispatcher. It was going to be a long day.

Alexis sat down on the bed next to Ricardo and wrapped her arm around his shoulders as the young man began to cry, first softly and then in loud, uncontrollable sobs. Finally he quieted down a bit and looked up at them, his voice shaking.

"How—how is Esperanza?" asked Ricardo.

"She's in the hospital now at Holy Cross," answered Alexis. She stood up and went to the window, and then she gestured toward the master bathroom. "She was physically and sexually abused and assaulted in that bathroom last night."

"I can't believe it," Ricardo said. "Is she gonna be okay? I mean, what you're saying is that she was raped, right?"

"Yes," answered Alexis, "she was raped, sexually abused, sexually assaulted, and hit in the head with what we believe was a hand gun."

Ricardo dropped his head back into the palms of his hands and sobbed. "My parents are gonna kill me," he wailed.

Chance stood in front of Ricardo, who was still seated on his parents' bed, and ask if he knew whether there were any University of Arizona students at his party the previous night. While Alexis recorded his answers, Ricardo said yes, there were a few U of A students present. Chance asked Ricardo if he knew them, if they were friends of his, and how many had been at his home. Ricardo told him there were probably five or six guys from the U of A and that he didn't know them very well.

"They are sort of friends of a friend," Ricardo said.

"Who's your friend that knows them personally then?" asked Chance.

"His name's Bryan Branoff. He's a senior at our high school and a friend of mine."

"Did Bryan invite them to your party, or did you?" Chance asked.

"We both invited them, I guess," answered Ricardo. "Bryan asked me if they could come, and I said yes because we all had met and hung out a couple of times together."

"Where did you hang out with these guys before?" Chance asked.

"They're all basketball players at the U of A. Bryan and I got tickets from them a couple of times and drove up there to watch them play, and then we hung out with them after the games at one of their apartments just off campus in downtown Tucson."

"Have you ever heard of one of them named Steven Styles?" asked Chance.

Ricardo's face went white, and he stared up at Chance. "Yeah, Steven Styles is one of them—he's the starting point guard for the U of A. Please don't tell me that he did this," pleaded Ricardo, throwing his head back and heaving a huge sigh.

"What does Steven Styles look like?" asked Chance. "Describe him for us."

"He's white, about six one or six two, probably weighs around two hundred pounds, and he has blond short hair and a blond mustache and goatee."

"Is he a friend of yours?"

"No, like I said, I've just watched him play basketball a couple of times, and he was at the apartment we went to after the games. He's a strange guy. I don't like him."

"Why don't you like him?"

"Because, like I said, he's strange. He's kind of a loner, kind of crazy, mean, and violent. I always stayed away from him because all the other guys say he's nuts and carries a gun or big Bowie knife with him all the time. I only met him twice, and I was kind of scared of him, so I stayed away from him. Everyone says he's violent and has a bad temper, so I stayed clear of him."

"Was Steven at your party last night?"

"Yeah, I saw him walk in with the others, but I stayed away from him."

"What others?"

"Some other basketball players from the U of A. Like I said, I really don't know them. I just got introduced to them a couple of times after we watched them play, that's all. They're not my friends or nothin'. I just know them from watching them play basketball and meeting them once or twice afterward at some dude's apartment off campus."

"Thanks, Ricardo, you did good. That's all for right now." Chance looked over at his detective. "I know you're tired, Detective Montoya, but do you mind going to interview Esperanza's two girlfriends to see what additional information they may have?"

"Not at all," answered Alexis. "I'll go right now and call you when I'm done."

"Good," said Chance. "I'll wait here for the evidence tech and help him process the bathroom. Ricardo, you're to stay here in your house. You won't be talkin' to no one on the phone or in person, either. Got it?"

"Yes, sir," answered Ricardo, with a look of complete terror in his wet, reddened eyes.

Alexis left the house once she had contacted Esperanza's two friends, Maria and Melinda, on her cell phone. She had arranged to meet with each of them separately at their homes. Both of the girls lived with their parents.

While Chance waited for the evidence tech to meet him, he continued to talk to and question Ricardo Rodriguez about anything and everything he could remember from the party the previous night, in an attempt to gather more information and to gain a better understanding of the series of events that had taken place on the premises. The more he talked with Ricardo, the more Chance's cop sense told him the kid was honest and telling the truth. Chance could tell Ricardo was genuinely concerned with and upset about Esperanza's welfare. The teen was completely cognizant of the circumstances that had occurred at his home the previous night and realized how serious the situation was, both for Esperanza and for him.

The evidence tech on duty for the day shift was Tom Bowers, who Chance had always liked and respected. Tom was an older deputy with twenty years of experience and a serious, professional demeanor. Chance felt comfortable with Tom's ability to process the scene and to obtain and secure the evidence they needed to help in identifying and convicting the suspect.

Chance met Tom at the front door of the house and led him upstairs to the master bathroom. Tom took a look around the room and sighed deeply, as if he were in remorse, and then he immediately and solemnly went to work. Tom had the unfortunate and somber experience of processing many violent crime scenes in his long career.

Chance instructed Ricardo to stay seated on the bed while Tom Bowers processed the scene and collected evidence. Chance acted as Bowers' assistant, working alongside him for the two hours it took to photograph the scene; dust it and obtain some partial and full finger prints; collect blood, semen, and hair samples; and collect all other physical evidence that would help tell the story of what had occurred in this room and clearly identify the suspect who had performed these dirty, disgusting, and dehumanizing deeds. That's one thing Sheriff Colt had learned very well throughout his twenty-five year career in law enforcement: the crime scene and its related evidence always told in gory detail the story of what had happened there. A crime scene never lied; it always told the truth. Unlike human beings, who often lied, the crime scene could be counted on to reveal the true tale and the facts of what evil acts had transpired inside its environs.

When Tom Bowers completed his work at the house, he informed Chance he would be heading back to the office, even though it was a Sunday, and would have his investigation and testing results completed no later than the first thing the next morning.

"Appreciate your dedication, Tom," said Chance. "Anything I can do to help, let me know."

After Tom left, Chance wrapped up his questioning with Ricardo and left him there, lonely and alone, to ponder his present and future circumstances. Sheriff Colt recommended to Ricardo he get in touch with his parents as soon as possible, so they would be aware of what had taken place in their home. Chance also recommended Ricardo and his parents contact and consult with an attorney, as they were most likely going to need one. Even though they didn't commit the crime, the rape had taken place on their property, which could possibly leave them open to civil or criminal liability.

Chance shook hands with the boy, who was still trembling, and thanked him, leaving Ricardo to wonder whether the seemingly simple act of hosting a party for his friends would have lasting ill effects on his and his family's futures.

"Bad things sometimes happen to good people," Chance explained to Ricardo, "but it's how a man handles adversity that shows his true colors and defines his true character." He gave Ricardo one of his business cards, told him to call if he remembered anything else, and wished him good luck.

Chance was dead on his feet tired when he got back into his truck. "No rest for the weary," he reminded himself. He called Alexis to see how the interviews were coming along with Maria and Melinda. Alexis said she had talked to both girls and hadn't learned much that was new. He told her to meet back at the station in Nogales when she had completed her work so they could share what information they had thus far regarding Esperanza's case.

When Chance arrived at his office, he removed his cowboy hat and boots, sank into his office chair, leaned back, and promptly fell sound asleep. He dreamt of Esperanza, Anna Antone, and the late, great Sheriff White, who had died in his overturned vehicle in the performance of his duty so long ago.

Chance awoke nearly two hours later to the sweet, sultry sound of Alexis' voice whispering softly into his right ear. He smelled her scent—some kind of women's body spray. He was so startled that he jumped to his feet, groggy and slow in identifying his surroundings and recognizing his friend, the sweet and sexy but tough-as-nails Detective Alexis Montoya.

"Did I scare you, Chief?" Alexis said, laughing playfully.

"No, you didn't scare me, you just surprised me," he stated with some embarrassment. "I was in the middle of a dream."

"Oh, you men and your sex dreams," Alexis said. "Who were you dreaming about this time?"

"You don't want to know," Chance stated matter-of-factly. "Take my word for it. You wouldn't like my dreams."

"While you were napping, I was out working on our rape case. Let me get us both a cup of coffee, and then we can catch up and compare notes. Do you want cream and sugar?"

"No, I like my coffee like I like my women: black." Chance smiled his sarcastic smile and sat back down in his chair. "And don't call me chief. I'm not an Indian chief," he hollered at her back as she left to get the coffees.

Alexis grinned at her boss as she returned to his office with two full, steaming mugs. It seemed to amuse her when she got a rise out of Chance simply by calling him chief, judging by how often she did it. She set the two cups of coffee on Chance's desk, sat down in one of his visitor's chairs, and propped her size six brown leather hiking boots up on the edge of Chance's desk, which she knew also annoyed him.

"Okay, Chief, what have we got so far?" she inquired with a devilish smile beaming across her pretty face.

"It's Sunday morning or afternoon, I'm so tired I don't even know which is correct, and we still got two dead Shadow Wolf Indians and a sexually abused fifteen-year-old Hispanic girl. I want both of these cases wrapped up in a nice little bow and solved before we get a return visit from the men in black on Monday—tomorrow. That's what we've got."

"The rape case is a slam dunk," answered Alexis. "All we have to do is wait for the physical evidence from Bowers to be completed and then go find the future wannabe movie star, current psychopath, and son of a bitch Steven Styles."

"As far as the two Shadow Wolf murders, we'll also get the physical evidence we need tomorrow. Then we can easily break Agent Anna Antone's resolve. She'll crumble like a Chinese fortune cookie."

"I like fortune cookies," said Chance. "I get some of my best advice from them." He took a long draught from his mug and immediately regretted it, since he burned his tongue.

"Both of these cases will be wrapped up and resolved by no later than tomorrow evening. Then the men in black will go back to Washington and all will be calm and quiet in sleepy Santa Cruz County, Arizona, once again," said Alexis. She leaned forward, offering her mug in a toast, and he bumped his mug against hers.

"In the meantime," she went on, "we call Black Chief with our updates and then we all go home and get some sleep for a change. Tomorrow, Monday, will be the day of reckoning for both Anna Antone and Steven Styles, and justice will be swiftly served. Piece of cake, Sheriff."

"I hope you're right, because this western lawman is gettin' too old and too sick and tired of this shitty world we live in—and just about everyone in it."

"Even me?" asked Alexis.

"No, not you." Chance yawned long and loud, not even trying to stifle it. "You and a handful of others can remain in my world. The rest may have to go away, though, so I can finally get some peace and quiet, not to mention some damn sleep."

Chapter Twelve

On his way home to his ranch house in Sonoita, Chance began to plan out tomorrow's activities, if all went well. Of course, his ever-present spirit guide, the dead Sheriff White, also chimed in with his thoughts and opinions on each of the cases. Through the years, Chance had often discussed his cases out loud with Sheriff White, and he wondered if that made him neurotic or crazy in any way. He decided once again it did not. As he well knew, many a human being received assistance and advice from the dead. Why should he be any different? He wasn't crazy, he was just using all of the resources available to him, whether they were dead or alive, part of this world or part of the spirit world.

Alexis could be as wild as a ricochet out of a loose cannon when it came to getting even with evil men, so he thought to himself that it would be best if she wasn't involved in the search for and arrest of Steven Styles. Alexis' skills and female charms would be better used in interrogating Agent

Anna Antone and getting her to confess to the murders of Billy Big Bear and Jim Walking Horse.

Chance decided he would get an arrest warrant for Steven Styles and complete that task himself. He would stop at the University of Arizona's registrar's office after getting the evidence tech's full report. The registrar would have Steven's address on file, and Chance would go to his address and wait for him to return home. He'd ask for backup from the university police or Tucson P.D., if he felt it was necessary.

When Chance arrived home, he had dinner with Sarah and man's best friend, Shakespeare. Then he prepared himself for his big day tomorrow by reading some of his favorite passages from *The Art of War,* written by the ancient Asian philosopher Sun Tzu. This, he thought, would put him in the proper frame of mind for his encounter and battle with the evil Steven Styles.

Heading out to the barn, he spent a few minutes with his horses before feeding and watering them. Stroking their silky noses and necks relaxed him, and he couldn't help taking a few minutes to toss the ball for Shakespeare too. Then he hit the hay early himself, so he would be refreshed and energized in the morning and be on top of his game for anything that might happen.

Being a lawman was a lot like being a Marine. In both professions, you always had to be prepared for anything and everything that might come your way. Without a moment's notice, the real shit could hit the proverbial fan.

The sun rose majestically on Monday morning over the eastern mountains. The sky was a pastel painting of shades of red. Chance woke to his old-man's alarm clock in his head, which didn't leave room for much else, he thought. It was precisely 0600 hours.

He got out of bed, let Shakespeare out for his morning "taking care of business," came back into the house, shaved and showered, and dressed in his khaki short-sleeved summer uniform shirt, dark brown uniform pants, black leather gun belt, and brown felt cowboy hat. It took him a few minutes to find his boots in the living room, where they had been unceremoniously knocked on their sides by the big oaf, William Shakespeare. He picked up one boot at a time, turned it upside down, and shook it three or four times before putting them on his feet. Being born in the American West, one learned early in life to shake out his boots before putting them on, to ensure no scorpion, rattlesnake, or other poisonous critter had borrowed them to use as a temporary home or hiding place.

He thought about taking his partner, Shakespeare, along with him today for work, but decided against it, as he reminded himself of the business at hand he had to attend to. He figured Shakespeare would be safer in the confines of the home ranch. No sense placing the dog in any danger, if it could be avoided. Shakespeare could come along on another, more routine, day.

"Red sky at night, sailor's delight; red sky in morning, sailors take warning," he said to himself as he looked at the fiery eastern sky. He had learned that saying when he was just a kid. His uncle had passed along the wisdom and lore he had learned from his years spent sailing the seven seas and travelling the world in the U.S. Navy. Chance's cop sense noted the sky's subtle warning and tucked it away in the recesses of his mind.

Chance walked toward the barn and heard the familiar nickers and whinnies from Butch Cassidy and the Sundance Kid. He said good morning to the two horses while he fed and watered them. When they were through with their breakfast, he gave them each a sugar cube treat that he had put in his pants pocket before leaving the house.

After putting their halters on, he walked the two horses out to the round training pen and let them loose. He watched them walk, trot, and lope around the corral for a little early morning exercise, marveling at their majestic beauty. Butch, Sarah's horse, was a six-year-old American quarter horse gelding, brown with a black mane and tail and a white diamond on his forehead that almost seemed to glow in the dark against the background of his deep brown, shiny coat. Sundance, Chance's horse, was a big, muscular, five-year-old brown and white paint gelding.

Both horses had been bought as young colts from a neighboring rancher and horse trader and started by Chance and Sarah. They believed in natural training and horsemanship, so their horses were humanely trained and started instead of being cruelly broken the old-fashioned way, with fear and intimidation. Chance and Sarah believed their horses would grow up to be calmer and more trusting after being trained in this way. In Chance's mind, one didn't own a horse; instead, a man or woman befriended a horse, and they grew in time to become partners together, each one holding an equal and mutual love and respect for the other.

The ringing of Chance's cell phone broke him away from his peaceful trance, as he watched the horses trotting and nipping each other playfully in the round pen. He saw Black Chief's number on his phone.

"Give me some good news, John," he said. "Did you finally get the search warrants from the judge for Anna Antone's truck and house?"

"Yep, I sure did," Black Chief replied. "It's time to do some searchin' and seizin' before the men in black beat us to it."

"I hear that, my friend," said Chance. "The good thing is the men in black are probably still trying to figure out where the reservation is. Unfortunately, I'll have to let you perform the search with Detective Montoya without me. I'm pretty busy following up on the rape of a fifteen-year-old girl over the weekend in Rio Rico. I'm going to get a warrant this morning to arrest the suspect, who's a U of A student up in Tucson."

"That works for me," said Black Chief. "Frankly I'd rather look at Alexis all day than stare at your ugly mug for ten seconds."

"You must've broke your last mirror my friend," Chance said with a chuckle. "I'll call Alexis now and tell her to call you, so you two can meet at Agent Antone's house and search the house and her truck. Just keep me informed of your progress, would ya?"

"Absolutely. The truck is where we should find the good evidence that will seal the deal. Then I'll turn Alexis loose on Anna and see if we can break her down and get a confession."

"If anyone can break her down, Alexis can. She's tough as nails and smart as the day is long. Keep me up to date, and good luck."

"Good luck to you too, Chance. And be careful with going after the rapist. I don't have to tell you those kind of men are always a little off-kilter. Make sure you're on your toes."

"I definitely will be careful, John. I'm gettin' too old to get outsmarted by some college-aged fraternity boy punk."

"Call me if you need any help, amigo," said Black Chief. "Otherwise we'll keep in touch with each other throughout the day. Happy hunting."

"Talk to you soon, John. I'll send Alexis your way now, but you two be safe too."

"I don't work it any other way, my friend. I'm gettin' too old too. We'll talk to you later," replied Black Chief. "It's going to be a good day for the good guys."

Chance hung up his phone and immediately called Alexis to fill her in on the day's agenda. "You meet up with John and work on the Anna Antone case. I'll take care of business up at the U of A with our basketball playing movie star. We'll keep in touch throughout the day," said Chance.

"That's probably the safer plan," Alexis said. "If I go up to arrest that scumbag rapist, I'll probably end up castrating the SOB on the way back down to the lock-up. Good luck and be careful. You know the guy is probably whacked out of his mind. Most rapists usually are."

"Keep me updated on your progress with Anna Antone and the search results," said Chance. "I'll call you as soon as I pick up Steven Styles. Talk to you soon."

After hanging up with Alexis, Chance stood by the round corral in the warm morning sunshine, watching the horses sun themselves. He called for the county's sketch artist, Manny Pablo, and asked him to meet at the Holy Cross Hospital at 0900 hours, so he could work with Esperanza to get a good sketch of her assailant. Chance then called the evidence tech, Tom Bowers, to see if he had any test results back yet from processing the crime scene the day before.

"Guess what?" Tom said. "It seems that our basketball star has a way with the young ladies—the very young ladies. I'd define it as a fetish for younger teenage girls. I found out that he's a suspect in two more rapes that occurred on campus with U of A students in the past six months. It appears our boy may be a serial rapist, according to my source at the university's police department. Only they don't have enough evidence to prove it yet. However, we do, thanks to yours truly."

"What have you got?" asked Chance, his heart racing. This was too easy.

"I've got full, clear finger prints that are an exact match to Steven Styles that were on file from previous arrests. I've also got pubic hair samples and the DNA from the semen samples found at the scene, which I'm willing to bet will match our friend Steven when we take him into custody and take samples from him. The blood samples found at the scene were all from Esperanza. However, the finger prints on the bathroom floor and countertop all are a definite match to Steven Styles. Once we match the pubic hair and semen samples found to Steven Styles, his goose is cooked. I have semen samples from both Esperanza's underwear and the tile floor."

"Good work, detective," Chance said to Tom Bowers. "I'm going to meet with Manny Pablo at 0900 hours at the hospital to get a good sketch of our suspect. Then I'm going to find a county judge willing to execute an arrest and search warrant on Steven Styles. Then I'm taking a drive up to the U of A on this fine Monday morning and try to locate Mr. Styles."

"Do you mind if I tag along on your trip up to the university?" asked Bowers.

"Not at all, Tom. I could use the good company. How about I pick you up at the station in Nogales around 1100 hours, after I get the suspect's sketch from Manny Pablo?"

"Sounds good, Chance. I'll be ready and waiting. I could use a day out of the office and lab and into some fresh air," answered Tom.

Chance hung up his cell phone, took one last long gander at his horses, and told them he hoped they'd have a good day at home on the ranch. Butch and Sundance offered a fond farewell whinny to Chance as he gave each horse another sweet cube of sugar as a treat for his equine friends.

Chance walked over to his Blazer, got in, and started up the engine of his steel, glass, and chrome version of a horse. He headed the old girl down the long gravel and sand driveway and pointed her in the direction of Holy Cross Hospital in Rio Rico. Between listening to his favorite radio station and the police scanner, the drive went quickly.

He met with the department's sketch artist, Manny Pablo, in the hospital waiting room. Chance politely asked Manny if he minded waiting a couple of minutes while Chance went into Esperanza's room to see how she was feeling this morning.

"No, man, I got nothin' better to do." Manny settled into a waiting room chair and pulled out his phone.

When he stuck his head in the door of Esperanza's room, he saw the teen's mom and dad sitting with their daughter. Chance greeted them and asked if he could join them, and they waved him in. He removed his hat and pulled up a chair next to Esperanza's bed, noting that she looked tired and subdued. She perked up a little when she recognized the sheriff's smiling face from the day before.

"How are you doing this morning, Esperanza?" Chance asked as he looked into the girl's young and innocent eyes.

"I'm a little tired and sore, but otherwise I'm okay," she answered with a half-smile of her own.

"If you feel up to it, I brought a friend of mine along by the name of Manny Pablo. Manny is an artist, and he specializes in drawing people's portraits. I was hoping you could work with Manny today, so he can draw a sketch of the man who hurt you. It will help us find him faster, if we have the sketch to show around. Does that sound all right with you?"

"Yeah, I can do that," answered Esperanza. "I have a good memory of what he looks like."

"Well, then, I'll go get Manny if this is a good time for you and your mom and dad. He's waiting just outside." Chance looked up with a smile and received verbal permission from Esperanza and a silent affirmative nod of the head from both her mom and dad.

"Good. I'll go get him and introduce you two." Chance stood up with his hat in his hands and walked out of the room while returning a polite nod of thanks to both Mr. and Mrs. Gonzales.

Within one minute, Chance walked back into Esperanza's room with Manny and introduced him to Esperanza and her parents. Manny was polite and professional, and sat down in the chair next to Esperanza's bed, speaking to her in a kind and soft-spoken manner. He showed her his sketch pad and his many colored pencils and explained what he was going to do. He would ask her some basic questions, she would answer them with her best recollection, and he would begin to draw his picture from there. Once he had a full description and Esperanza's approval of his drawing, he would make several copies from the nurse's copy machine and give one to Chance. Esperanza agreed to do her best, and the sketch process began.

After about an hour had elapsed, Manny had the sketch completed and had received Esperanza's stamp of approval. Manny quickly made copies at the nurse's station, and Chance had several copies of the sketch in hand. Manny and Chance thanked Esperanza for her great help and stated they would let her get some more rest and spend time with her mom and dad. Chance asked Esperanza if it was all right for him to stop by toward the end of the evening, so he could see how she was doing, and she readily agreed with a smile.

"Do you want me to bring you anything?" Chance asked.

Esperanza smiled shyly. "How about maybe a chocolate shake with whipped cream and sprinkles?"

"Consider it done," Chance said. "Maybe I'll bring two—one for you and one for me. I have a craving for a chocolate shake too. Just don't tell my wife, okay? She'll be mad at me if I have one without her."

Chance put on his cowboy hat, said his goodbyes to Esperanza and her parents, and promised he would be back later that night with the chocolate shakes. With that, he gave a two-fingered salute and touched the brim of his hat before walking purposefully and quickly out of the hospital room.

Once outside in the parking lot, Chance met up with Manny Pablo once again, thanked him for his help, and jumped into his truck. His next stop would be the station in Nogales and the courthouse to obtain his search and arrest warrants for Steven Styles.

He arrived at the Sheriff's Station around 1100 hours and found evidence tech Tom Bowers ready and waiting for him.

"Let's go to the courthouse ASAP so we can catch a judge before they all take off on their two-hour lunches," Chance said to Bowers.

A half hour later they had explained the case and evidence to Judge Earl Monroe and had an arrest warrant in hand for Steven Styles, along with a search warrant for his residence and vehicle.

Chance was in a hurry to get up to Tucson and locate Steven Styles, so he and Bowers stopped quickly at a local hot dog stand for lunch and wolfed down a couple of Sonoran dogs each, washing them down with an ice-cold bottle of Coca-Cola. Chance then filled up the old Blazer with gas, and they drove up to the University of Arizona in Tucson.

They stopped at the U of A registrar's office to flash their badges and sweet-talk the secretary into giving them Steven Styles' address and a copy of his student photo ID. Then they were on their way to stake out the premises and wait for Styles to come home from his Monday classes at the university. Chance had obtained a copy of Styles' class schedule from the nice secretary at the registrar's office as well, so they had a good idea when Styles would be returning home to his off-campus apartment after attending, somewhat ironically, his abnormal psychology class. It seemed a fitting omen and metaphor, Chance thought.

As Chance and Detective Bowers waited in the parking lot of the apartment complex for Styles to return home, he called Alexis for an update on the Anna Antone house and truck search. He also placed a courtesy call to the University Police Department. In just a few minutes, if all went well, he was going to make an arrest on their turf.

Chapter Thirteen

"Good afternoon, Sunshine," Chance said into his cell phone. Detective Montoya was on the other end of the line. "How's the truck and house search coming along?"

"It's going well," answered Alexis. "Did you arrest that Steven Styles son of a bitch yet?"

"Tom Bowers and I are staking out his apartment as we speak. We're waiting for him to get out of his abnormal psych class, of all things."

"You've got to be kidding," said Alexis. "How ironic is that?"

"That's what I was thinking too. Styles probably knows enough about the subject matter that he could teach the class or just stay home and study himself in the mirror. What have you and Black Chief got so far?"

"We brought Mike Munoz with us to collect evidence, and we've already struck gold with Anna Antone's pickup," Alexis said. "The tire treads on her truck match the tracks we found at the murder scene. And even though Anna apparently tried to erase any physical evidence from the truck with a thorough car wash, Mike has already found traces of both Billy Big Bear's and Jim Walking Horse's blood in the bed of her rusty old pickup. No matter how hard people try, it seems they can never quite get rid of minute traces of blood. Isn't modern science and technology a marvel and a police officer's best friend?"

"No," said Chance, "my Glock sidearm is my best friend. Well, my gun and the great William Shakespeare, of course, but that goes without saying."

"Men and their dogs and guns," responded Alexis with a long sigh.

"Like my grandfather always used to say, 'A man only needs four things in life to be truly happy: a good woman, a good dog, a good gun, and a good truck.' And three out of four ain't bad," Chance said with a chuckle.

"Whatever, Sheriff," Alexis said impatiently. "Anyway, getting back to reality, we've still got Anna Antone's house to search, and we're looking for Dorothy's magical ruby red slippers, size seven, in the form of a pair of Dan Post cowboy boots. If the boots match the crime scene prints and fit Anna's Antone's feet, I'm going to kick her in the ass with them."

"I love it when you talk dirty. Who's Dorothy?" asked Chance with a sarcastic laugh. "The murderer's name is Anna."

Chance could hear Alexis rummaging through Anna Antone's house as she spoke. "Well, what do you know? Look what I just found in the back of Anna's bedroom closet," Alexis said aloud. "A dirty and dusty pair of black Dan Post cowboy boots, size seven. I think we'll finish up with the search of the house and then go back to the station and interview Ms. Antone again with our new-found knowledge."

"Make sure her lawyer is present to be a witness to his client's unfortunate news."

"No worries, Sheriff. I think we'll be tying this case up with a pretty red bow in a few hours, just like you hoped," stated Alexis. "I've got to let you go now. All this hard evidence is making Agent John Black Chief hungry, and I promised to buy him lunch at a little café in Ajo before we head back down to talk to our prisoner in Sells."

"Happy trails to you," Chance said. "Keep me posted on how the interrogation goes."

"Absolutely, Sheriff. Keep me posted on when you arrest the sick son of a bitch who hurt poor little Esperanza."

"Roger that," said Chance. "I'll be calling you soon, hopefully."

"Be careful, and don't call me Roger." Alexis laughed and hung up the phone.

Chance pocketed his cell phone and settled in to wait with Bowers for Steven Styles to arrive home from class.

After they had sat waiting in the hot Chevy Blazer for almost an hour, a University of Arizona police cruiser pulled into the parking lot of the apartment complex and parked right next to Chance's vehicle.

"Oh, great," Chance growled. "The Welcome Wagon is here to blow our surprise."

A Hispanic police officer got out of his car and nonchalantly walked up to Chance's open window. The name tag on his uniform shirt said Officer Sanchez. "Good afternoon, Sheriff Colt. Thanks for the courtesy call. I was told to come and assist you with your arrest."

"I didn't ask for any assistance," said Chance. "I just called as a professional courtesy to let you guys know we were here. I don't want Steven Styles coming home and seeing a police parade outside his apartment. I kind of wanted to take him by surprise. Why don't you move your cruiser, so we're not so obvious?"

As the words came out of Chance's mouth, a shiny black Dodge Challenger came barreling into the parking lot with music blaring from the open car windows. In the driver's seat sat a young blond-haired man matching the description of Steven Styles. He rolled up the dark tinted windows, shut off the ignition, exited the vehicle, and stared down Officer Sanchez, Detective Bowers, and Sheriff Colt as he slammed his car door shut and strutted like a male peacock toward his apartment building.

"Well, so much for our surprise," said Chance, as he and Bowers exited the Blazer. Chance and Bowers started to follow Steven Styles to the door of his apartment, with Officer Sanchez right behind them.

"Spread out a little," Chance told Bowers and Sanchez. "This guy is known to carry a gun, and right now with you two so close to me, he could take all three of us out, like we were three dead ducks in a shooting gallery. Give me some space and let me do the talking. You two just watch his hands and make sure he keeps them in our sight at all times."

Chance was right behind Steven Styles by the time he reached his apartment door and put his key in the door lock. Styles unlocked and opened the door but didn't make an attempt to step inside. Instead, he quickly turned to face Sheriff Colt.

"What can I do for you, Officer?" asked Styles, with a broad smile widening across his face.

"I'm not an officer, Steven," said Chance. "My name is Sheriff Colt, and I came up here from Santa Cruz County to talk to you."

"About what?" Styles asked sarcastically, with the big, fake smile still plastered onto his face.

"I'd rather talk to you inside. Do you mind if we come in?" asked Sheriff Colt.

"Yeah, as a matter of fact, I do mind," answered Styles. "I'm kind of busy at the moment. Maybe you gentlemen can make an appointment with my secretary and come back another time when you're invited." Styles stood face to face with Sheriff Colt, invading the sheriff's personal space.

"I hate to interrupt your busy schedule, Steven, but I am invited." Chance put his right hand on Style's chest and pushed him out of his way and into the darkness of the apartment. "I have a warrant from a judge that says I'm invited, if you'd care to read it."

"A warrant for what?" Styles snarled, as he steadied himself from being pushed into the living room of his apartment by Sheriff Colt.

"A warrant to search your apartment and a warrant for your arrest, if need be," Chance growled back. All three police officers were now inside the apartment.

Detective Bowers fumbled to find a light switch on the wall so they could clearly see the premises they were now blindly entering. Bowers finally located a switch and turned on the light.

"Do you live here alone, or do you have a roommate?" asked Chance, as he once again distanced himself from the other two police officers out of habit and learned survival skills.

"I live alone," Styles said, "but that doesn't give you the right to barge right in, and it certainly doesn't give you the right to push me."

Chance's eyes adjusted to the light, and he quickly took in his environment and surroundings with all of his senses, as he kept his eyes fixed on Styles' empty hands.

"I have the right to do whatever I want, Steven. Now, do you want to calm down and sit down and talk to us politely, or do we have to do it the hard way?" the sheriff demanded, as the blood in his veins began to turn that familiar dead calm cold, and his gut told him something bad was about to happen.

Styles' face was red with anger, and he appeared to be mentally calculating his options as he glared at Sheriff Colt.

"Well, what's it gonna be, Steven?" demanded Chance.

"Fine," Steven said, visibly working to appear calm. "We can sit and talk, but I have to take a piss first." He turned and briskly walked into the bathroom and shut the door behind him.

Chance, Bowers, and Sanchez looked around at the apartment, which Chance thought was way too neat, clean, and organized for a normal college kid living on his own. Chance saw various stacks of porn magazines and videos, including child pornography, in neat rows on several book shelves. Styles had enough material to open up his own porn shop, Chance thought, as he looked around the room at the shelves, a big-screen television, a computer and monitor sitting on a desk in the corner of the room, a couch and two reclining La-Z-Boy chairs that faced the T.V. There was also a small kitchen with a table and two chairs. Further down the hallway from the bathroom that Styles had rushed into was what appeared to be the one and only bedroom.

"Check the bedroom," Chance barked to Bowers, as he instinctively drew his Glock pistol from its holster and took cover behind the kitchen cabinets and countertop. Officer Sanchez stood unmoving and frozen in the middle of the living room floor, and he looked at Chance with a somewhat perplexed and confused expression on his face.

Chance's heart quickly turned to stone as he felt a sudden and familiar chill enter the room. The bathroom door swung quickly open, and the sheriff raised his firearm with both hands in a ready-to-fire defensive position in the direction of the opening door.

A gunshot exploded from the bathroom and struck Officer Sanchez in the head as Styles entered into the living room in a flash, continuing to fire shots at random around the room from his 9mm pistol. Sanchez's body immediately dropped to the floor, the police officer dead before he even hit the ground, with blood and brain matter splattering onto the white wall behind him like red paint.

Styles turned his attention and firearm toward Chance with his eyes ablaze with angry, devilish hell-fire. Chance stood up from behind the kitchen counter and fired his Glock three times center-mass into Styles' chest. For a brief instant, Styles and the sheriff locked eyes on each other in a demon-like death stare, and Chance fired his weapon one more time, the .40 caliber round hitting Styles in his throat and jaw. The younger man's jugular vein exploded into a bloody mist of spraying flesh, blood, and bone that splattered onto Chance's face and body.

Styles' dead body slumped to the floor, landing with a dull thud. Chance immediately picked up and secured the dead man's weapon, turned the lifeless body over onto its back, and quickly checked the wrist for a pulse. As Chance had suspected, any sign of life was absent; the young man had bled out quickly. He stepped over to Sanchez and found the same lack of vital signs. Chance would be calling the coroner rather than the ambulance.

Chance looked into the face of Steven Styles, or what was left of it, once more, and glared into the dead, open eyes with an animal-like hatred radiating from his own burning eyes. Chance slowly regained his composure and returned the Shadow Man quietly and calmly back into the inner recesses of his heart and soul, where it would live a dormant and peaceful life again.

"It's safe to come out now, Bowers," Chance called loudly toward the bedroom, as he stared with a blank expression on his face at the dead rapist lying at his feet. Bowers stepped out of the bedroom and back into the living room, staring wide-eyed at the dead bodies of Steven Styles and Officer Sanchez and the blood-spattered face of Sheriff Chance Colt.

"Are you hurt?" asked Bowers, his face appearing as white as a ghost.

"Nope," answered Chance quietly, without looking up.

"What should we do now?" asked Bowers, with a look of complete shock on his face.

"My recommendation is to dial 911 on your cell phone, so someone can come and clean up this mess," Chance answered calmly, coldly, and without emotion.

"Yes, sir, Sheriff," replied Bowers, and his trembling hands reached into his pocket for his cell phone.

Chapter Fourteen

"Well, it's about time you called me," said Detective Montoya. "While you and Bowers have been leisurely sightseeing up in Tucson all day, I've been interrogating Ms. Anna Antone."

"How's it going?" asked Chance.

"Great. Wonderful. I got her to make a complete confession to both murders—signed, sealed, and delivered. Case closed, and I'm sitting at the station writing my novel of a report that's going to take me days to complete, with no help from your lazy ass. How's our son of a bitch rapist, Steven Styles?"

"Dead," said Chance.

"What?" asked Alexis.

"Steven Styles is no longer a member of the human race."

"Seriously?"

"Serious as a heart attack," replied Chance.

"What happened?"

"I killed him," answered Chance. "That's it. Just like you, case closed. Unlike you, I think I'll write my novel of a report tomorrow. Right now, I'm going home to take a shower, clean myself up, and go buy two chocolate shakes. Then I'm going to go visit a little fifteen-year-old girl at the hospital in Rio Rico, like I promised her I would this morning. You can fill me in on all the details of the Anna Antone case and confession tomorrow morning. Right now, I have a date I need to keep with Esperanza."

Chance hung up his cell phone, and he and Bowers, exhausted physically and drained emotionally, walked out of the University of Arizona police station. For the past several hours they had endured extensive, exhaustive questioning by U of A detectives on the shootings in Steven Styles' apartment that had ended with the fatalities of Officer Sanchez and Steven Styles. Apparently they had satisfied the U of A police regarding the circumstances resulting in the two deaths, and they were pronounced free to leave.

One of the U of A detectives gave Chance and Bowers a ride back to the Blazer, which was still parked where they had left it earlier in the afternoon in the parking lot of the dead man's apartment complex. Chance and Bowers shook hands with the U of A detective as they thanked him for the ride. They exited the unmarked police cruiser and walked back to the Blazer. Chance started up the truck and drove back to the I-19 freeway. As they headed south toward home, neither man uttered a single word. Both were quietly lost in their own recollections of what had taken place earlier in the day.

Chance dropped Bowers off at his unmarked car in the Sheriff's Department in Nogales. They shook hands, said good night, and went their separate ways after promising to touch base with each other in the morning.

As Chance drove home alone in the darkening silence of another southeastern Arizona day, he heard the distinctive voice from the past coming from the back seat of the Blazer.

Don't let killing a man bother you, said the dead Sheriff George White from the great beyond. *If anyone deserved to die, it was Steven Styles.*

"I know," agreed Chance. "It just never feels good when I have to play God and take another man's life."

You weren't playing God, Sheriff Colt, replied the voice. *You were performing and carrying out your job and your duty.*

"I guess so," Chance said, "but I can never find any solace or peace in taking another human being's life. God knows, I've had to do it enough times in war as a Marine scout sniper and in my career as an Arizona lawman. It just never gets any easier. All it does is add one more dead man's ghost to the long list of other dead men's ghosts that will haunt me until it's my turn to die. Death seems to surround me and follow me like a black rain cloud wherever I go. I'm tired of all the sadness, death, and killing in my life. I'm sick and tired of my job, but there's nowhere I can escape to where I can find lasting peace. I can run, but I can never hide. The dead won't let me live my life in peace. Maybe I'll only find true peace in my own death. In the meantime, I try to find as much happiness and peace as I can among the living. I just hope God forgives me come judgment day."

He already has forgiven you, Chance! exclaimed White. *Don't you see you are doing God's work for him while you walk upon His earth? And come judgment day, a man like you will be rewarded by God, not punished. Know that, and you will know peace.*

"I hope you're right, Sheriff White," whispered Chance in a dry and hoarse voice, "because if you're wrong, I am going straight to hell."

Trust me, said the voice. *Trust Him.*

Chance drove the rest of the way home to his ranch in Sonoita in deep silence and thought. When he reached his driveway, he stopped to look at the sign overhead that he had made with his own hands so long ago. It read, "The Sanctuary Ranch." Reading it and looking out over his home, his barn, his corrals, his pastures, and his hundred acres of land, he began once again to find some small amount of peace inside his own self-made sanctuary.

As Chance walked into the house, Sarah looked up at him and must have noticed his blood-stained uniform. She gasped, and her face fell. She got up from her rocking chair to greet him with a hug, as tears fell down her cheeks.

"Are you okay?" she asked, with her head buried deep in his chest.

"I'm fine," he answered. "It's not my blood. It looks worse than it actually is. I just need to get out of these clothes, take a hot shower, and clean myself up so I can feel like a human being again."

William Shakespeare looked up at Chance calmly and knowingly with wise old eyes. The dog appeared to nod his head up and down in an all-knowing nonverbal message to Chance of his understanding, knowledge, peace, and love. The look Shakespeare gave him was a reassurance that all was well in the world. Chance petted Shakespeare in a quiet moment of thanks, understanding, and appreciation, and he then began removing all of his blood-stained clothes. He handed the pile to Sarah and said, "Burn them. Burn them all in the fireplace. Ashes to ashes; dust to dust."

Chance walked naked upstairs and into their master bathroom. He heated up the shower until it was steaming, and then he stepped under the water jets and rinsed his body clean of the blood. In a way, he felt he was also cleansing his soul of sin.

Once out of the shower, he dressed again in blue jeans and a black County Sheriff's Department t-shirt. He found Sarah and told her about his promise to visit Esperanza at the hospital before his long day could finally be over, after which he could come home, once again, and get some much-needed sleep.

He picked up two large, ice-cold chocolate shakes at a drive-through in Rio Rico and made his way to the hospital. He found Esperanza resting comfortably and watching T.V. with her parents in her room. She sat up in bed and smiled with delight, as Chance handed her the chocolate shake she had been craving and waiting for all day. Chance spoke with Esperanza and Mr. and Mrs. Gonzales about the teen's school and her friends and about his dog and his horses, being sure not to speak of any of the real events that had transpired earlier that day.

After about an hour, Chance stood up, placed his cowboy hat back on his head, and told Esperanza and her parents that he would come back to visit again tomorrow. Then he wished the young and innocent Esperanza a good night and sweet, chocolate dreams.

On his way out the hospital room door, he caught the eye of Mr. Gonzales and motioned with his head toward the outside hallway. Esperanza's parents followed Chance out into the hall, and he shut the door behind them before quietly informing them that he had shot and killed the suspect in Esperanza's rape, a man by the name of Steven Styles, from Tucson. He reassured them that their daughter would no longer have to live in fear of this evil man ever again. He advised them to do everything in their power to help their daughter put this horrifying incident behind her, and to concentrate on Esperanza's healing. He was certain, he told them, that she would soon become a happy, healthy, well-adjusted teenage girl once more.

Mr. Gonzales thanked Chance and shook his hand tightly, tears in his eyes. Mrs. Gonzales hugged the sheriff, thanking him and crying tears that were a mixture of pent-up feelings and emotions from the past two days.

With a final goodnight, Chance headed for the hospital exit. He drove straight home to his Sanctuary Ranch in complete silence. Despite the late hour by the time he got to his own driveway, he stopped by the barn to check on the horses before going inside the house. Finally, he entered the log cabin, undressed, and climbed into the bed he shared with his wife, enjoying the warmth and comfort radiating from Sarah's and Shakespeare's sleeping bodies.

I may be dead tired, but I ain't dead, he thought. It had been a day of one more win for good over evil. "Forgive me, God," were the last words whispered out of his mouth before he fell into a deep and peaceful sleep.

Chance awoke on Tuesday morning to the warm Arizona sunshine illuminating his and Sarah's bed. When his eyes popped open, he promptly received a wet good-morning lick on the cheek from his dog. He found his wife in the kitchen and gave her a warm good morning kiss before letting Shake and Bake outside to do his thing, and then he walked over to the barn to feed and water Butch and Sundance. He walked the horses out to the round corral and let them run and play to their heart's content.

Back inside the ranch house, he shaved, showered, and dressed in his uniform in anticipation of another eventful day—though not as eventful as the previous day, he hoped. Today was the day he would meet with Alexis to go over the wrap-up of her Shadow Wolf murder investigation and report. With some luck, today also would be the day they could say goodbye to Agent Ryan and his men in black. Chance could hardly wait to send them all packing and on their way out of Santa Cruz County and his life.

When Chance arrived at his office in Nogales, he found Alexis and Agent Ryan, with his men in black, already waiting for him. He invited his detective and the lead federal agent into his office and left the remainder of the feds cooling their spit-shined heels out in the lobby with Shirley.

"Good morning, Detective Montoya and Agent Ryan," he said, closing the office door for privacy. "Since you're both here, I thought you, Alexis, could brief both Agent Ryan and me together on the conclusion of your investigation in the last couple of days with the arrest and confession of Agent Anna Antone for the murders of Shadow Wolf agents Billy Big Bear and Jim Walking Horse. Pardon the poor pun, but I figured we could kill two birds with one stone, so to speak, and save Alexis explaining her work twice."

"That would be fine with me," said Agent Ryan, "if it's okay with you, Detective Montoya?"

"Anything to save time," answered Alexis. "I'll start off with obtaining and executing the search warrants for Agent Antone's pickup truck and home. Agent-in-Charge John Black Chief and I were able to get the search warrants from the tribal judge yesterday morning. We searched the suspect's Ford F-150 pickup truck first with our evidence tech, Mike Munoz. Mike was also the E.T. who initially processed both murder scenes. The truck tire treads matched exactly the tire tracks found at the scene of the murders. The Evidence Tech was also able to obtain traces of blood samples of both victims, Billy Big Bear and Jim Walking Horse, from the bed of Antone's pickup truck that matched the blood found at the murder scene and the blood of both victims. You could tell Anna Antone had attempted to wash and clean the truck to eliminate evidence, but you know, Agent Ryan, how difficult it is to get rid of all traces of blood.

"While searching Antone's house, we found a pair of Dan Post cowboy boots, size seven, in the back of Anna's bedroom closet that matched the footprints found and preserved at the murder scene. The dust and mud we found on the boots also was consistent with the dust and mud taken as samples from the crime scene.

"After we performed the search on the truck and house, we seized and impounded the vehicle and had it delivered to our evidence storage facility. We also took the cowboy boots and secured them as evidence, after we had Antone try them on. She actually admitted they belonged to her. She didn't seem to care about implicating herself."

"After the searches were completed, I Mirandized and interrogated Anna Antone with her lawyer present, where she subsequently admitted to committing the murders of both Billy Big Bear and Jim Walking Horse."

"She actually confessed?" Chance let out a long, low whistle and scratched his head. "And her lawyers let her do that?"

"Yes, she did, and they couldn't stop her, although they tried," Alexis said. "It was almost too easy. After I explained to her all of the evidence that was collected at the crime scene, in her truck, and at her residence, Anna broke down and told us everything. We have her written and signed statement, as well as audio and video of the interrogation and confession that she agreed to allow us to record in advance."

"What was her motive for murder?" Ryan asked.

"We had suspected it was based on relationship issues, and we were right," she told him. "Antone admitted to having a sexual relationship with Agent Billy Big Bear for the past eighteen months, while simultaneously having an affair with Agent Jim Walking Horse for the past twelve months. Antone stated that neither man was aware of the simultaneous affairs until recently. When the men found out, they both attempted to end their relationships with Antone. She stated that she threatened to tell their wives about their sexual affairs with her if they broke it off, after which both Billy Big Bear and Jim Walking Horse threatened to kill her if she followed through."

"Antone then stated that she feared for her own life based on those threats, and she decided to plan and carry out the murders of both men before they had the chance to kill her. She set up what she called a final date off of the reservation with both men in the town of Tubac, where they went out for dinner and drinks at Elvira's Restaurant & Bar. She stated she got both of the victims drunk on Long Island Ice Teas and had used one dose of the drug Rohypnol, otherwise known on the street as "roofies," that she had mixed into the men's drinks when they went to the restroom. She admitted to driving both men out to the same location a day apart from each other, where she hanged the men with a rope from a mesquite tree and then drove her pickup truck from underneath them to break their necks or cause them to choke to death from hanging.

"After she thought the men were dead, she drove her pickup truck back underneath the bodies of the hanging men and used a hunting knife to cut off the men's penises and testicles and place them in their mouths. A hunting knife with traces of blood on it was found behind the seat of Anna's Ford F-150 during our search of the vehicle at her residence. The knife has been booked into evidence, as well.

"The motive for these murders, Anna claims, was her fear that Big Bear or Walking Horse would kill her if she didn't kill them first. Her motive for cutting off the left hand ring fingers and wedding bands of both men and mailing these items to the victim's wives was retribution and revenge, and what Anna is claiming was temporary insanity. She wanted to send an anonymous message to each wife to let them know that their husbands were cheating on them.

"And that pretty much wraps up both murder case investigations. After the interrogation, Anna was formally charged with both homicides. She's currently being held in the Tohono O'odham Indian Nation jail in Sells, waiting to be transported to the Santa Cruz County jail for her initial court appearance and arraignment. Any questions?" Detective Montoya looked back and forth between Sheriff Colt and Agent Ryan.

"Yeah," said Chance. "Why in the hell did she cut off their penises and testicles?"

"Because she's nuts and wanted revenge," answered Alexis.

"Works for me," said Chance. "No other questions from me, Detective. Excellent work on both of these investigations. I knew I could count on you to solve these murders quickly. You're the best there is, so congratulations on a job well done. Agent Ryan, do you need anything further from us? It seems like we've wrapped up these two investigations for you, the FBI, and ICE."

"I agree, Sheriff. Job well done, Detective Montoya," Ryan said. "On behalf of the Federal Bureau of Investigation and the Immigration and Customs Enforcement Agency, I'd like to thank you for your quick and thorough investigation and assistance. Sheriff, I'd like to personally thank you too for your work and cooperation. You've made our job here a lot easier. It was a pleasure working with the both of you. I guess we'll be on our way then."

"Hold on, Agent Ryan," said Chance. "It's Tuesday and time for my Buddhist meditation class again. Would you guys like to hang around and go with me again tonight? I know how much fun you had last week."

"No thanks, Sheriff," Ryan said with a laugh. "Our one session with you last week was enough. I've received all of the inner peace I need for a lifetime from that one class with you."

"Just keep in mind what my grandfather always used to say," Chance said with the straightest face he could muster. "It's an ancient Buddhist proverb: If you meet the Buddha on the road—kill him."

"Uh, right, got it. That's good advice, Sheriff," said Ryan, and Chance could tell the fed didn't get his joke. "Thank you, and may the force be with you, or whatever you Buddhists say to each other."

"That's actually a line from *Star Wars,*" Chance said, "not a Buddhist saying. Don't you ever get out and have fun?"

"My mistake—and no, fun is an unnecessary waste of time when there's work to be done. That's how we do things in Washington. We'll be on our way now and out of your hair." Ryan stood up and hurried out of Chance's office, and that was the last that was seen of the men in black in Santa Cruz County, Arizona, for some time.

Chapter Fifteen

After Agent Ryan and his men in black left the sheriff's office and headed back to Washington, Chance and Alexis both heaved a sigh of relief at the same time. Then they laughed together as Chance wiggled his eyebrows. Alexis asked Chance for the details from the previous day's attempted arrest and shooting of Esperanza's rapist, Steven Styles, up in Tucson.

"You know I don't like to kill and tell, Alexis," answered Chance. "Let's just let dead men lie for now, shall we? We both have reports to write and finish up, so we should get to work on that. You can read my report when it's finished. That should answer your questions and give you all the details you need. I'm not much of a talker, you know."

"That's putting it mildly," said Alexis, "but I know what you mean—silence is golden. I'll be at my desk putting the finishing touches on my novel. Let me know if you want to do lunch."

"Lunch would be good," Chance said. "How about around noon, if we're both done with our reports?"

"Noon is good with me," answered Alexis. "Mine will take longer than yours, though."

"Do the best you can and shoot for noon. Close my office door on your way out, please."

"Yes sir, Sheriff," replied Alexis, as she stepped into the doorway. "By the way, you've got to work on the loner part of your personality. How did you ever get elected so many times when you're such an introvert?"

"I'm just lucky, I guess," replied Chance. "Maybe my actions speak louder than my words."

"What?" said Alexis. "I can't hear you."

"Exactly," said Chance.

Chance spun around in his desk chair to get a blank police report, so he could begin to write down his story of yesterday's unfortunate series of events—traumatic events that still sat heavy on his mind. He wanted to write it, forget it, and move on to the next chapter in his life. He glanced at the old *Life* magazine poster that hung on the wall behind his desk, and he read again the magazine's original motto, written by its founding fathers in 1883: *To see the world, things dangerous to come to, to see behind walls, draw closer to find each other and to feel... That is the purpose of life.* Even after all of these years, Chance believed in the beauty of these simple truths and tried to live his own life by them each day, to the best of his abilities. Reading these old, wise words once again lightened his darkened mood somewhat and renewed his spirit, his faith in his life, and his purpose for walking the path that he had chosen so long ago.

He immersed himself in writing his report, determined to tell the truth, the whole truth, and nothing but the truth, so help him God, until he had it completed. He purged himself of the events as he wrote. Finally, more than an hour later, he signed his name to it and handed it to Shirley to process and file. With that deed done, he cleared the incident from his mind, and that act in itself made him feel clean once more.

He glanced at the clock and saw that it was just past noon. He walked into Detective Montoya's office. She was busily typing on her laptop and glanced up when he came in.

"How's that report coming along?" he said. "Ready for lunch? Cuz if you ain't, I'm goin' without you, I'm that hungry."

"You bet I'm ready," she answered. "What do you have a taste for?"

"Anything," said Chance. "You choose."

The two of them walked out of the Sheriff's Station into the bright afternoon sun. Alexis insisted on driving, since the place she chose was a diner across town. Chance felt a little guilty about filling up on a double cheeseburger and fries, deciding he'd cut back on dinner or run around the round pen with the horses for some exercise, to make up for it. They made light conversation about their families, Chance avoiding any talk of the details of the shootings.

After lunch, Chance jumped into his Blazer and headed up to Rio Rico and Holy Cross Hospital to visit Esperanza and her parents. On his way up I-19, Chance had the truck humming along in the right-hand lane at a smooth sixty-five miles per hour, enjoying the scenic desert and mountain vistas of what was commonly called in these parts the Borderlands Region.

A red Porsche 911 convertible with California license plates flew by him in the left-hand lane, travelling at least one hundred miles per hour with the top down. The car wasn't the only thing with its top down, he noted. In the split-second flash of red, as they blew by him in a blur, he saw a young, attractive blond man driving and an equally attractive blonde woman occupying the passenger seat of the sports car. The woman appeared to be stark naked, wearing nothing but a pair of dark sunglasses and a smile.

As soon as the driver of the Porsche saw the county sheriff star and logo on the side of the Blazer and the emergency light bar on the roof, he slowed down to the legal speed limit of seventy-five miles per hour. Putting on his right turn signal, he maneuvered the Porsche into the right-hand lane.

"Damn Californians think they can do whatever they want when they want," Chance said aloud. "The land of fruits and nuts and egos the size of the Goodyear blimp, including all the hot air to go along with it." He hit the gas and flipped on his lights and siren, deciding that he should catch up to Flash Gordon and his titty-flashing female companion.

Immediately, the sports car slowed down and began to pull over to the right shoulder of the highway. After it came to a complete stop, Chance called in his traffic stop to Shirley. "California plate, Charles, bravo, ocean, nine, one, one."

Shirley repeated the license plate number and instructed Sheriff Colt to stand by while she ran it through the computer. Chance waited patiently for Shirley's response.

"Santa Cruz to Unit 10."

"Go ahead, Santa Cruz," Chance responded.

"The plate comes back clear and valid to a Chad Brian Osbourne out of Beverly Hills, California, date of birth 10/18/82."

"10-4, Santa Cruz. I'll be 10-6 for a few minutes," Chance said into the mic of his Motorola radio.

"10-4, Unit 10."

"Why is every guy from Beverly Hills named Chad?" Chance questioned himself aloud, as he unbuckled his seat belt and exited his vehicle. The date of birth and the name itself fit the driver, but you could never tell for sure till you saw the license. The car could have been stolen by these kids for a joy ride. *A naked woman usually equals joy,* he thought.

He walked up to the Porsche along the passenger side of the vehicle with his left hand on his Glock .40 pistol grip for two reasons. First, to protect himself from accidentally getting struck by oncoming traffic, a tragedy that killed many police officers every year; second, to get a good look at the naked, good-looking young blonde, who was now attempting to put on her bra and panties.

"No need to get dressed on my account, ma'am," Chance said politely, touching the brim of his hat. She was stunningly beautiful, even while struggling to cover up and put on her undergarments. She flashed him a golden Hollywood smile and finished fastening her bra and pulling up her white lace panties, both of which still left little to Chance's imagination. She didn't bother to reach for the rest of her clothes. She sat there in the passenger seat unmoving, quiet, and still smiling politely at the sheriff, as if she were posing for a *Playboy* magazine photo shoot.

"Sir, do me a favor and turn off your ignition and place both of your hands on the steering wheel, where I can see them clearly." asked Chance.

"Yes sir, officer," answered the driver, as he placed his trembling hands on the steering wheel and gripped it tightly.

"I'm not an officer, I'm the Santa Cruz County Sheriff. Do you know how fast you were going, sir?"

"Uh, yes sir, I actually do, Sheriff," the young man answered. "Truthfully, I thought your truck was so old that it was an antique vehicle made up to look like a police vehicle. How old is that thing?"

"So you know you were going at least a hundred miles per hour, then?" asked Chance.

"Oh, yes sir. I was going at the very least a hundred miles per hour."

"Where's the fire, chief? Why are you driving so fast?"

"Uh, just enjoying the day, I guess."

"What brings you two from California to our fine Grand Canyon State?"

"We're just visiting for a few days. You know, sightseeing and visiting old friends."

"You'd both see a lot more of Arizona if you'd slow down a little, don't you think?"

"Yes sir, Sheriff." The driver nodded vigorously. "You're absolutely right. Sometimes I just let this baby get away from me without noticing it."

"Can I see your license, insurance card, and vehicle registration, slowly with one hand, please?"

"Of course, Sheriff. Don't worry, it's not like I'm gonna shoot you or something."

"That's what the last guy that shot me said," Chance said. "From then on, I kinda lost my trust in human nature."

The driver reached for his wallet in his rear pants pocket, took out his driver's license, and handed it to the sheriff. He was indeed Chad.

"Honey, can you open the glove box and give the sheriff my vehicle registration and insurance card, please?" Chad said, as he motioned to the beautiful blonde.

"And what's your name, Miss?" Chance watched her open up the glove compartment door and reach in. She handed Chance the vehicle registration and insurance card.

"My name's Candice. Candice Connolly." She gave him another Hollywood-white smile with perfect teeth.

"Candice, do you have any identification you can show me?"

"Sure." She reached into her purse, retrieved her driver's license, and handed it to Chance.

"Candice Connolly from Hollywood, California," Chance said aloud as he quickly read her name from her ID. "Are you a movie star, Miss Connolly?"

"Um, sort of, I guess. I do porn films." Candice grinned cheerfully.

"That doesn't surprise me," replied Chance. "You are a very beautiful woman. In California, you might as well make the most of it, right? I wish you great success in your career choice."

"I'm trying to break into real films," Candice said in an apologetic tone, "but it's really hard to get a break."

"I'd think a young woman with your beauty should have a good chance." Chance handed her driver's license back to her. "I wish you all the best, ma'am." He looked over at

Chad and said, "You sit tight, Mr. Osbourne, and I'll be right back with your documents."

He quickly walked back to his vehicle and verified all the information with his dispatcher. Everything came back clear and valid to Chad Brian Osbourne of Beverly Hills, California. Chance exited his vehicle and walked back to the passenger side and the lovely Ms. Connolly. He handed all three documents over to Chad. Then he looked down at the long, tan, shapely legs belonging to Candice and drank in her natural beauty one last time.

"You two caught me in a good mood and on a good day," Chance said. "Enjoy our beautiful state during your visit, just do me a favor, Chad, and lighten up a little on the lead foot, okay? I'd hate to see either of you get hurt."

"Thank you, Sheriff," Chad and Candice replied in unison.

Chance tipped his cowboy hat at the young lady. "You two be safe now, ya hear?"

"Yes, sir," Chad replied, while Candice gave the sheriff one last movie star smile and a wink from her beautiful, baby blue eyes.

"Enjoy your day." Chance nodded, smiled, and quickly walked back to his truck. He watched the California couple slowly pull away and into the right lane of I-19 north again, while he grabbed the mic of his radio.

"Santa Cruz Dispatch, this is Unit 10 and I'm 10-8, back in service, and on my way once again to Holy Cross Hospital in Rio Rico."

"10-4, Sheriff," answered Shirley. "You say hello to that sweet little girl from all of us here at the station."

"I definitely will, Shirley. I'll talk to you later." Chance started up the Blazer and continued on his way in the warm afternoon sunshine of the Arizona borderlands.

A true Buddha lives in the present moment, Chance reminded himself. *A true Buddha lives in the now. The only time there is, is the time it is right now. Now see, you just missed it, didn't you? That moment has slipped past, and you are presently in a new now.*

If you want to observe and learn from a perfect Buddha, spend some quality time with a dog or a horse. Each animal is always living in the present moment. Each animal only knows and understands the now. A dog or horse doesn't dwell over its past or waste precious now time worrying about its future. All it feels, knows, and understands is the now.

Chance had spent the last couple of hours talking with Esperanza, her parents, her doctors, and her nurses. She was physically healthy and well enough to be discharged from the hospital tomorrow and go home to carry on with the rest of her life; however, it would take much longer to heal emotionally and psychologically from the trauma she had experienced.

This is why Chance felt the need to invite Esperanza and her parents out to his ranch, the Sanctuary, to spend a little time with his dog, William Shakespeare, and his horses, Butch Cassidy and the Sundance Kid. He was certain such a visit would assist her with healing from her emotional and psychological wounds.

Chance knew Esperanza would return to school and to her normal life, but not without the need for time to heal on the inside, in her heart, her mind, and her soul. He knew she would probably end up seeing a professional psychiatrist or therapist who would help her to understand and find her way through the emotional and psychological maze of recovery from the trauma she had experienced and endured.

He knew this firsthand, from his own recovery from his experiences with trauma after coming back from war during his days as a U.S. Marine. He had also experienced and lived through similar traumatic experiences and recovery of healing physically, emotionally, and psychologically from the physical and emotional wounds he had suffered as a lawman over the past twenty-five years.

Chance knew pain. It was, at times in his life, his closest companion and friend. Chance also knew something about healing and recovery. For these reasons, he had felt compelled to reach out with compassion to Esperanza and allow her the healing experiences of spending time with his dog and his horses at the Sanctuary Ranch.

Chance knew a little about the relatively new fields of dog and horse-assisted psychotherapy. He had studied the subject somewhat. He was definitely no doctor, psychiatrist, or professional therapist, but he had grown up with animals all of his life and personally experienced their healing powers. He had no grand illusions of being a healer or teacher himself; he just thought he could offer to be the go-between and open the pathway for Esperanza to work with the real teachers and healers of broken emotions, hearts, and souls: his four-legged friends. Inside each individual dog and horse seemed to dwell a mentor, and Chance knew that these humble animals sometimes had a deep knowledge and wisdom. He knew they could, at times, be the pathway for one to be led and guided by and used for healing and recovery purposes. And he knew sometimes these four-legged creatures could be the ones to lead others to the spiritual wisdom and spiritual peace of God himself.

Chance understood and knew in his heart and soul that all animals had a special relationship with God the Creator and the Spirit of all things, in this world as well as in the great beyond. And he felt compelled to offer this opportunity and path to Esperanza, by allowing her the chance to spend some quiet, peaceful, and meaningful time with his dog and horses, to gain back some amount of inner peace, happiness, wisdom, and contentment in her young life.

It was Tuesday evening, a little before 1700 hours, and time for Chance to work on his own inner peace and contentment with his life. It was time, once again, for his meditation class at the Empty Brush Sangha Buddhist Meditation Center in Tubac.

Chapter Sixteen

Chance arrived at the Buddhist Meditation Center and quickly changed into his Zen meditation robe, eager to start tonight's meditation practice. He had some tough inner work to do to lift the heavy weight of the killing of Steven Styles from his mind. The needless death of the campus police officer weighed heavily on him too.

When the bell rang softly three times to begin the session, Chance started his meditation off by apologizing to God and asking forgiveness for what he had done. He didn't like to take another human being's life, but he had done it in self-defense, and he had done it as a matter of duty in performing his job as a lawman, as a peaceful warrior and as a servant of God. It wasn't a sin—it was a matter of restoring good over evil. Steven Styles was an evil human being, a predator who preyed on helpless and innocent young girls. This world needed to get rid of evil spirits such as Steven Styles, and Chance just had the unlucky task of playing the exterminator. It was his duty; it was his calling; it was his job to rid this world of demons like Steven Styles.

And, like it or not, he knew he was good at it. He'd been good at it in defense of his country in war, as a Marine scout sniper, and he'd been good at it as an American lawman for the past twenty-five years. Someone had to take out the garbage, and for some reason, God had chosen him. Chance didn't have a choice in the matter. It was his destiny, and he must endure through it—not for himself, but for the Higher Power who had entrusted him with performing such a cold-blooded task.

This Chance believed in his mind, heart, and soul to be complete truth; a universal truth, communicated straight from God in heaven to him.

Therefore, he released the evil Steven Styles from his conscience and let him float away into the dark and unknown depths of hell. He released the evil and once again embraced the good. He thought only of Esperanza and concentrated his thoughts on her glowing and pure innocence and goodness, and his destiny to deliver her from evil and return her to inner peace and a lifetime of happiness and contentment.

When the bell rang once more to signal the end of his forty-five-minute meditation, Chance continued to sit in silence, extending his time of prayer and meditation for another hour or so. Finally he and the visiting Buddhist monk who had supervised today's class were the only two people left in the meditation center; everyone else had gone home for the night. When Chance opened his eyes, he saw sitting directly across from him the smiling, peaceful Buddhist monk. No words were exchanged between the two men. No words were needed. Chance could feel the quiet, confident compassion radiating from this holy man and encircling Chance with a forgiving, peaceful and radiant blue light that penetrated his own heart, mind, and soul.

The monk and Chance exchanged smiles and a knowing nod. Both men slowly rose from their sitting positions, walked to the locker room in complete silence, and quietly changed back into their street clothes. They walked out of the temple side by side, bowed a silent good night to each other, and separated into the quiet star-filled night with a sense of stillness, peace, and compassion for each other and for all mankind.

Chance drove home in his old truck with the windows rolled all the way down, feeling as though he were an eagle feather floating on the warm breeze of a quiet, serene Sonoran desert night. Nothing disturbed his tranquility; his meditation had taken care of that.

He awoke in his own bed the next morning with a clear conscience, a warm feeling in his head and heart, and a feeling of true happiness and contentment for himself and for Esperanza. The circle of life continued to spin in abandon, wild and free into the unknowable future.

Summer monsoon season had come and gone, and Chance's life went on without hearing a word from Esperanza or her parents. It was now late September and Esperanza was probably busy with her junior year of high school and all of the things associated with it.

One day, out of the blue, Chance decided to call Mr. and Mrs. Gonzales to see how the teenager was doing. He was saddened to hear that she hadn't fared well in the months since the rape. Her parents described her as quiet, sad, and withdrawn—not the talkative, sociable, happy young girl she had once been. Her grades at school were suffering, and she was spending too much time brooding silently alone in her bedroom, seemingly lost in her own thoughts and lost to the outside world.

"I know a little bit about how to fix lost souls," Chance told them. "I was one too, a few times in my life. I'd like to reiterate my offer of having the three of you come out to my ranch and meet my wife, my dog, and my horses. I think it would do Esperanza a world of good. How about you all come out for the day this Saturday, and we can talk and spend some time together. I'd like to see Esperanza and try to help her sort out her feelings. With your permission, of course," Chance emphasized. "I think it's worth a shot, and I think I know someone who can help her out of her funk and become the old Esperanza again. What do you say?"

Mr. and Mrs. Gonzales agreed that such a visit might help Esperanza, so they readily accepted the invitation to the Sanctuary Ranch on Saturday. Chance and Sarah would provide lunch, and Esperanza would meet William Shakespeare, Butch Cassidy, and the Sundance Kid.

"You can tell a lot about a person's character by observing and getting to know his four-legged friends," Chance told Esperanza. They were sitting together on the wide, shady porch of the ranch house while her parents had stepped inside to visit to meet Sarah. "Dogs and horses also have a keen sense of awareness and can sometimes help the character of a human being that is in need of some guidance and help. Dogs and horses embody the knowledge and wisdom of God in their minds, hearts, and souls, Esperanza. I really believe it, because I've seen it with my own two eyes."

Esperanza looked at Chance with quite a bit of doubt and suspicion. "How do you know that?"

"Well, take William Shakespeare here, for instance," Chance began, as he playfully petted his middle-aged black Lab and introduced Esperanza to him. "Go ahead and pet him and talk to him. He won't bite. He looks tough, but he's really a big, lovable softy at heart. Do you have any pets of your own, Esperanza?"

Esperanza reached out to William Shakespeare and patted his head, then sank her fingers into the silky fur of his neck and chest. Soon Shakespeare was sitting next to Esperanza, leaning his full body weight against her, enjoying his massage.

"My mom and dad haven't let me have any pets, but I'd love to have a dog someday," Esperanza said. "I've never been around a dog this big. How much does Shakespeare weigh? He feels heavy, leaning all his weight on me the way he is." She smiled for the first time since she and her parents had arrived to the ranch.

"That means he likes you and trusts you," Chance said. "He weighs about one hundred and ten pounds. He'd let you give him a free massage all day if you were willing. He loves the attention. He always wants to play the happy clown and steal the spotlight and be the center of attention."

"I like dogs," she said simply.

"Do you trust me, Esperanza?" asked Chance, as he looked straight into the teenager's dark brown eyes.

"I don't know," answered Esperanza. "I guess I do—I mean, you are the sheriff and all. I just have a hard time trusting anyone, since my, you know—incident. I've kind of closed myself off to people since the rape, I guess. I know my mom and dad say that you can help me, but I don't really know if you can. They tried taking me to a special psychiatrist after the school psychologist and the psychiatrist at the hospital. I didn't like talking to them. No one knows what I've been through, and everyone judges me and has an opinion of me, but none of them can understand how I feel inside or how I can live with the pain, fear, and guilt."

"What if I told you that I live with pain, fear, and guilt too, every day of my life, since I returned home from being a U.S. Marine in war time when I was a young man, and all through my law enforcement career, up until this very day?"

"I'd believe you," answered Esperanza. "My mom and dad told me you've been through a lot of difficult times in your life too."

"I have," answered Chance. "And I've learned through my life that sometimes other human beings can't help me; most other people just can't relate to my experiences. They've never been there, done that—know what I mean?"

"Yeah, I do," Esperanza said with a look of sadness and frustration, as she continued petting Shakespeare.

"But that's the difference between animals and people," Chance said. "Animals seem to have a closer relationship with their own kind and other animals' feelings, including us human beings. They can't talk our language, but they can communicate nonverbally with us, and they have a sort of innate wisdom and intuitive sense that people just don't have. Sometimes I think animals have a closer relationship with God."

"Maybe." Esperanza kept her eyes and her hands on Shakespeare. The dog rolled over onto his back, with his legs and belly up, allowing the girl to scratch his belly.

"That means he trusts you too," said Chance. "Dogs are natural predators, and they have their own survival instincts and fear other predators, just like human beings. He wouldn't expose his belly and throat to you like that if he didn't trust you. However, in this short time we've been talking, ol' Shake and Bake has sensed he can trust you. He's read your nonverbal cues and body language, and he's come to the conclusion that he can trust you."

"That's good. I like him too."

"Sometimes I wish people were more like dogs. Dogs don't know how to fake it or lie; they only know sincerity and truth. And Shake and Bake has tested you and judged you, and decided he can trust you, all in a matter of minutes. I think you've made a new best friend."

Hearing these words from Chance, Esperanza sighed and said, "I can use a friend right about now. I think I like dogs more than I like people. In fact, I pretty much hate people."

"I sometimes feel the same way too, Esperanza. I definitely felt that way when I came back from war as a young man. I've also gone through phases as a lawman where I've pretty much hated and distrusted all people. People like us, who've had bad things happen to us in our lives, need to learn to trust again. And since many people aren't very trustworthy, sometimes it makes more sense for people like you and me to start building trust again with animals first. After all, what does 'dog' spell backwards?"

Esperanza appeared to be mulling over the thought in her mind. "God?"

"You've got it," said Chance. "Like my grandfather always used to say, 'Dog spelled backwards is God. Think about that, and treat them accordingly.'"

Hearing this from Chance, Esperanza's face broke into a big smile. "I like that," she said. "God spelled backwards is dog, and dog spelled backwards is God." She giggled for the first time in months, and her laughter caught the attention of her mom and dad, who were just stepping out onto the porch. They smiled a friendly smile of parental relief as they both nodded their heads in a silent thanks to Chance.

Esperanza's laughter and smiles also infected Shakespeare, who got up and ran around Esperanza in circles, with a goofy smile of his own on his face. He dashed into the yard, found his bright green tennis ball, and dropped it at her feet. Thus began a game of catch and retrieve with the teenager for the next few minutes, before Esperanza had tired old William Shakespeare out. He ran to his water bowl, gulped up some cool, fresh water, and collapsed on the front porch of the house to catch a quick afternoon snooze in the shade.

Esperanza watched Shakespeare get a drink and lie down for a nap on the porch, and she absentmindedly smiled from ear to ear. So did all of the rest of the relieved adults present—Mr. and Mrs. Gonzales, Sarah, and Chance. William Shakespeare had, once again, worked his four-legged magic to lighten the mood of all and spread his complete happiness in the now of the present moment, until it had infected the minds, hearts, and souls of everyone.

In the late afternoon, as Esperanza and her mom and dad were getting ready to head for their home, Chance gave Esperanza another gift to look forward to. "Next time you come to our ranch to visit, I want you to meet two more of our four-legged friends, our horses, Butch Cassidy and the Sundance Kid."

"Can I come back, Mom and Dad?" Esperanza asked with a wave of happiness and excitement enveloping her entire face.

"Of course you can come back," answered her mother, as her dad nodded in agreement with a grateful smile, "as long as Sarah and Chance invite you."

"How about next week on Saturday?" Chance said.

"Sounds okay with me." Esperanza smiled breathlessly and looked toward her parents for their approval.

"It's a date," said Mr. Gonzales.

The Gonzales family said their goodbyes to Sarah, Shakespeare, and Chance and hopped into their truck for the ride home to Rio Rico. Before getting in the truck, Mr. Gonzales pulled Chance aside, shook his hand firmly, and smiled a knowing grin with his eyes filling up with tears of joy. "Thank you, Sheriff. You don't know how much this day has meant to me, my wife, and especially Esperanza. I sincerely thank you with all my heart."

"I do know what it means, Hector. I've been where Esperanza is right now. It's a dark and lonely place to be, but we can't let her remain there forever. I think with the help of Shakespeare, Butch, and Sundance, we can bring your little girl back to you and your wife again. In fact, I know we can. And please call me Chance. I'm not offering Esperanza help as a county sheriff; I'm offering her our help as fellow human beings, along with our four-legged friends. Your daughter deserves a second chance at a happy life, and Chance is who I am and what I do. I offer second chances to those who need it most."

Chapter Seventeen

"The Buddhist religion teaches that you have to admit you're a fool before you can truly become wise, Chance said to his young visitor. They were sitting on the porch of his ranch house on a lazy Saturday. The day couldn't be more perfect: a cloudless sky, mild temperatures for Arizona, and no urgent calls—for the moment. "My name is Chance, and I'm a baboon. Now you say it, Esperanza."

Esperanza laughed aloud. "My name is Esperanza, and I'm a baboon!"

"Very good, fellow baboon. You've now successfully mastered step one to becoming a fully enlightened human being and wise beyond your years." He gave her a playful pat on the back. "I have a book I'd like you to read. It's called *Tao Te Ching and the Art of Harmony,* and it was written thousands of years ago by a mythical author named Laozi. This book isn't like your typical, boring high school text book.

I guarantee it'll teach you things you could never learn in any normal school about living in harmony with yourself, your life, your world, and everyone in it. What do you say—would you like to read it?"

"Sure. I mean, I guess so," Esperanza answered. "It sounds more interesting than any of my high school text books."

"Good, I'll loan you mine today. I also want you to meet our horses, Butch Cassidy and the Sundance Kid. Butch is Sarah's horse, and he's a gelding American quarter horse. Sundance is my horse—he's a gelding paint, which means he's white with spots or patches of another color, in his case, brown patches. They're going to teach us a little bit about the art of living in harmony too. Are you ready to go meet them?"

"Absolutely," Esperanza said. "I just have one question: what's a gelding?"

"Oh, right, I should explain that. Just like all animals, there are male horses and female horses. When a horse is born, it's either a male, which is called a colt, or a female, which is called a filly. At around the age of three or four, a male colt is usually castrated to settle him down somewhat. Once he loses the family jewels, he's called a gelding and is easier to train. So a gelding is just a castrated male horse. If he wasn't castrated, he would be called a stallion. When a stallion is used for breeding purposes, it's called a stud. They're usually a lot harder to train than a gelding and a lot more stubborn, wild, and spirited."

Chance led Esperanza to the open barn door, with Shakespeare tagging along. The horses began to nicker their greeting to the visitors. "That's a horse's way of communicating a friendly hello to his two-legged friends," Chance explained to Esperanza.

Chance led each horse, one at a time, out to the round training pen. Butch and Sundance came nose to nose with Shakespeare in their friendly animal greeting, sniffing and licking each other. Then they nuzzled their heads into Chance's shoulder and neck in their own version of a gentle horse hug.

Once the horses were secured in the round training pen with the gate closed, Chance, Esperanza, and Shakespeare watched the horses trot and lope around the corral, stretching their strong, athletic legs.

"Horses are a bit different than dogs," Chance began to explain to Esperanza. "Remember when I told you that dogs are predators?"

"I remember," replied Esperanza.

"Well, horses are generally considered to be herd animals and fall into the prey category. My grandfather always taught me that there are really just two types of animals who live in this world: those that are natural predators and those that are natural prey. He also taught me that you can easily tell whether an animal is a predator or prey by the placement of their eyes. Predators have their eyes set in the front of their heads, which provides them with keen eyesight to see and identify their prey. For example, man is a predator, a mountain lion is a predator, and a wolf is a predator. They all have their eyes set in the front of their heads, which assists them in seeing, identifying, and capturing or overtaking their prey.

"On the other hand, animals included in the category of prey have their eyes set on the sides of their heads. Some examples of natural prey are fish, cattle, deer, big-horn sheep, and buffalo. How about the horse, Esperanza? If you follow my grandfather's rule of thumb, what is a horse, predator or prey?"

"I guess they would be prey, because their eyes are set on the sides of their heads, right?" Esperanza stood with one foot up on the bottom rail of the round pen, her arms draped over the top and her chin resting on her hands. She looked the picture of peace and contentment.

"You've got it," Chance said. He took off his hat and swiped his arm across his sweaty forehead. Although it was early October, the weather had warmed considerably over the past hour. "And because prey animals have their eyes set on the sides of their heads, their eyesight isn't as keen or as sharp as the sight of a predator, so that makes them vulnerable. Prey can be and often are attacked and killed by predators in the wild. It's a perfect example of survival of the fittest at work in the real world, and I'll bet you learned about that in science class at school, right?"

"Yeah. Your grandfather sounds like he was a pretty smart guy."

"That he was," said Chance. "My grandfather also taught me to never stand in front of a bull or behind a horse. If you mess with a bull, you get the horns. If you stand behind a horse, out of his line of sight, he's liable to get spooked and kick you in the head. Take it from me, getting kicked by a horse isn't much fun. I've learned that lesson the hard way a few times in my life. So since prey animals have to learn to protect themselves, they often become herd animals strictly for survival reasons. As herd animals, horses form natural friendships with their own kind—other horses. And they tend to be wary and suspicious of other animals, at least till they can build a relationship of trust. Horses kind of have to be admired and loved from a distance at first, before they learn they can trust you and you won't hurt them. When they learn to trust, they let you into their hearts and minds with the realization that you're a nice person and maybe even a friend they'll allow to join their herd. And once you're in their herd, you're in for life. Pretty cool, huh?"

"That's cool," said Esperanza. "You have to slowly earn their trust, just like with people."

"Exactly. Horses, just like people, learn who they can trust and who they can't trust. And like I said, once you earn their trust, you have that trust and friendship forever, as long as you continue to treat them right. If a person betrays their trust, it'll be hard for them to earn it back again. Horses don't forget stuff like that; it's pure survival instinct. With people, you build trust one person and one day at a time. With horses, it's the same thing; you also build trust one horse and one day at a time."

"That's pretty smart," she said. "I like that, and the way you explained it makes perfect sense, but I have some questions."

"Let's hear them."

"Well, you said that man is a predator. Do you mean all men and women? I don't feel like I'm a predator—I feel more like prey." She shrugged and gave a deep sigh. "I mean, I don't think I could attack or hurt another human being or even an animal."

"I sure do understand what you mean," Chance said. "I guess it would be more accurate to say that every man and woman has the ability to become a predator, but not all human beings will become one. Human beings only become predators out of necessity or by personal choice. Human beings have something called free will, but horses don't. It's a natural instinct or a learned and trained response for people. So, I guess, to answer your question fully, all men and women have the instinct or ability to be predators. However, most people—

like you—choose not to become predators, while others make a personal and conscious choice to become predators."

"Like Steven Styles?" asked Esperanza, catching Chance off guard with her question.

"Well, yes, like Steven Styles. For one reason or another, Steven made a conscious choice to become a predator. And that's what made him do the bad things he did. However, Steven freely chose his own fate."

"I'm not sorry for what happened to him," she said simply. She smoothed back her hair, which was twisted in a long braid that fell below her shoulders. "So, why did you decide to become a predator?"

"I guess I chose it out of choice, chance and circumstance, and out of necessity, due to my line of work."

She looked him directly in the eye. "I know you killed him, you know," she said in a voice so low it was almost a whisper.

"You know I killed who?"

"I know you killed Steven Styles. My mom and dad told me."

Chance decided to be direct. This girl deserved the truth from him. "Yes, I killed Steven Styles, but I did so out of necessity. He shot and killed another police officer when we went to arrest him. He was going to shoot me next, but I shot him first in self-defense. Again, it's part of my job, part of my duty as a lawman."

"Is he the first person you ever killed?"

"No," Chance said.

"So you've killed others?"

"Yes, I've killed others as a U.S. Marine in war and as a county sheriff."

"What's that like? I mean, how'd it make you feel?"

"That's a tough question for me to answer, and one I've struggled with answering my whole life. The closest I can define the truth is, it makes me feel bad at first, but then I'm able to rationalize it and it makes me feel better. I do it for a higher calling, a higher good. I do it in self-defense and to defend innocent people like you. I do it because it is the job God gave me to do. And I believe God will be the final judge of what I've done in the end. I'll have to answer to Him, and I'm at peace with that."

After a long, awkward moment of silence between the man and the teenager, Chance asked, "How about we get back to a lighter subject, like horses?"

"Sounds good to me," Esperanza said. "I just want to say that I really appreciate you talking to me, and especially the way you talk to me like an adult. It's been a tough year for me, and I know you have more important things to do as sheriff."

"Nothing is more important to me than your welfare, Esperanza. Believe me, I've been through some tough times myself in my life, and I consider it my duty and my personal honor to help you where I can, not just as a county sheriff but also as a fellow human being. We all need help sometimes with things in life, and we all need someone we can talk to. Believe me, I need someone to talk to, so you're helping me as much as I'm helping you. We're just two human beings helping each other get through this crazy maze called life."

Just then Sundance trotted over to the rail where they stood and stuck his nose over toward Chance. He patted the horse, and it wheeled and trotted away. "So, like my grandfather used to say, there are basically two kinds of horse and animal people in this world: those that get it and those that don't. And just like us human beings make judgments of other people, horses make judgments of other human beings and animals too. They either learn to trust you or they don't."

"I hope your horses will trust me," she said, watching them cavort in the round pen. Sundance nipped at Butch's hindquarters and nearly got kicked in the head before he dashed away.

"The old way of breaking a horse was to tie him down, basically roping all four of his legs, then get him to the ground and hold him there until you break his spirit and he gives up. That's a pretty traumatizing way to teach a horse or any kind of animal, isn't it? The horse, just like a human being, will never forget that trauma. It will scar him physically and emotionally for life."

"That sounds really mean," she said. "Like, I'd never do that to a horse, ever."

"I don't like it either," Chance said. "The new, more modern and humane way of training and mentoring a horse is to start him. We start horses by building a relationship based on love, trust and mutual respect. This is a much better way to treat and teach a horse, or any other animal for that matter, us human beings included, don't you agree?"

"Yeah," Esperanza said. "Who wants to live with fear and mistrust all the time?"

"Nobody," Chance said. "So what do horses and all animals fear? They're afraid of predators that could hurt or kill them. They're afraid of bright lights, loud noises, threatening body language and movements. If they get hurt, the actual incident or their recovery from that incident can stay in their memory and cause pain and suffering for the rest of their lives."

This seemed to resonate with Esperanza, as he heard her sniffle a little. She looked away from him and blinked fast, as if there was something in her eyes. He went on more gently.

"What do human beings fear? The same things; we fear predators that could hurt or kill us. We fear pain and loss of control. We fear unexpected incidents or events that can and do stay in our memories and cause pain and suffering for the rest of our lives. So horses, other animals, and people aren't so different in many respects. We're all related, we're all God's creatures, and we all fear and crave many of the same things. We have to learn to build trust with each other with love, compassion, and loyalty, not hatred, fear, and pain. Loyalty, love, and compassion for each other is the only way and only path to pure truth, peace, and happiness in this world for us all. Make sense?"

"Yeah. I hate the way people hurt each other," she said, anger tinging her voice. "I wouldn't hurt anyone, and I don't understand hurting animals either. Especially animals like these, like your horses. They're so beautiful."

"Well, the old way of breaking horses is mostly gone because it doesn't work. The new way of teaching and training horses is called natural horsemanship. It's about building a relationship of security, trust, love, and compassion. So how do we fix broken human beings? The same way we fix broken horses: by mentoring and teaching them with feelings of security, trust, love, and compassion. These four virtues are universal to the happiness and mental and physical health of all of God's creations, whether two-legged, four-legged, or winged, as the American Indian cultures and ancient Eastern philosophies all believe. These four universal truths—security, trust, love, and compassion—are the only natural truths inherent in the lives and spirits of all living things. Only when we realize and understand this will there be universal and true peace for us all in this world."

"How do you know so much?" Esperanza asked. "Are you some kind of teacher or priest or something too?"

"Nope," he laughed, "just a country sheriff. So, enough about all of this deep and philosophical thought. How about we go and play with the horses now?"

"Sounds good to me," Esperanza said with a genuine look of happiness on her face. She looked to Chance like she was about to start hopping up and down in excitement. "How do we start?"

"We start by introducing ourselves and sayin' hello to Butch and Sundance, and we build a relationship of security, trust, love, and compassion one day at a time, one horse at a time and one human at a time."

"Okay, but I'm confused. I don't know how to do that." She gazed over the top rail at the two horses, as if willing them to come to her.

"We'll go into the corral with them, into their comfort zone, and let them smell, touch, and feel you. Start just like you did with Shakespeare. Let Butch and Sundance smell the back of your hand and the rest of you. Horses have a strong sense of smell. Don't be afraid of them because they can sense fear, and that'll just make 'em nervous and fearful of you, as well."

"I'm not afraid of them. How could I be? I love them!" she breathed.

Chance opened the gate and walked inside the round pen with her. He began to coach her through the steps necessary to make friends with each horse.

"Slowly begin to touch them, softly and gently, with your hands. Horses also have a strong sense of touch and will respond positively to you and your touch if you move slow and deliberate, showing them they got nothin' to fear. Start with their head and neck and slowly work your way back, rubbing 'em, petting 'em, and gently touching their whole bodies.

"Talk softly and calmly to 'em while you do this. When they trust you as a friend, they'll begin to seek you out and come to you, rather than you coming to them. They'll come to you for your loving touch and your calming and compassionate words, as any other friend would."

Chance snapped a rope lead onto Butch's halter and handed the end of the rope to Esperanza.

"After spending some time just touching, smelling, feeling, and talking in a calm and reassuring manner, we begin to walk with them. Hold the lead and then walk them around the corral with confidence. Soon you won't even have to use the lead because they'll follow you on their own accord, without you having to pull them along."

She did as he said, and he couldn't help the silly grin that appeared on his face. She was a natural with the horses.

"Lastly, we'll saddle them up and get you used to sitting on their backs. Of course these guys are already used to having riders on them, but they'll sense that you're new to this. Then, finally, we'll have you ride them at a walk, then at a trot, and then at a lope or a gallop. Again, the whole relationship is built on trust and compassion. And I can tell, Esperanza, that they already trust you."

For the next several months, Esperanza spent most of her free time when she wasn't in school with Chance, Sarah, Alexis, John Black Chief, William Shakespeare, Butch Cassidy and the Sundance Kid. She learned, loved, laughed, and healed harmoniously, with the help of all of the sentient beings on the Sanctuary Ranch, both the two-legged and the four-legged. On most occasions, her parents Hector and Esmeralda joined in on the fun, the freedom, and the time of healing and maturing alongside their beautiful daughter.

Esperanza's transformation during those months was remarkable to watch, and Chance and Sarah spent many hours discussing how she had turned back into a happy, healthy, peaceful, confident and fun-loving teenager. It was almost like watching a true miracle in the making. It had been a long, difficult, and sometimes emotionally heartbreaking road to recovery and a difficult life journey, but one that was well worth the trip. Esperanza had fought hard, persevered, healed, and recovered. She had, with the assistance and natural animal wisdom of Shakespeare, Butch, and Sundance, made it all the way back to her rightful place as a normal, well-adjusted human being once again.

Who says you need a psychologist or psychiatrist when our Creator gave us dogs and horses? Chance thought. *Those critters are the true healers.*

The Arizona spring had sprung into the heat of summer. Esperanza had completed her junior year of high school and was anticipating the enjoyment of her last summer before entering her senior year. She would then head off to college and the joyful living out of the rest of her life, with the pain and hurt of her traumatic adolescent experience behind her for good and, hopefully, forgotten.

Chance had secretly asked Esperanza's parents for their permission to let him buy Esperanza her own horse for a birthday present, and Hector and Esmeralda had heartedly agreed. Chance assured both of them that her horse could be boarded and taken care of at the Sanctuary Ranch for as long as Esperanza wanted to keep him there, with no strings attached. She would be welcome to come and ride him and groom him any time that she wished.

With everyone's permission and delight, Chance, Sarah, Alexis, and Black Chief scoured southeastern Arizona for the right horse, until one day they found the perfect match for Esperanza. Rising Star was a glistening black five-year-old American quarter horse gelding, tall at sixteen hands and sporting a white five-point star on his forehead. He had the disposition of a peaceful and enlightened Buddhist monk or an American Indian medicine man. To be more accurate and precise, he was to become Esperanza's medicine horse, who would help her in continuing on her journey and path toward peace, happiness, and contentment, with herself and with her life for years to come.

On Esperanza's seventeenth birthday, with her parents and all her new-found friends—Sarah, Alexis, Black Chief, Shakespeare, Butch, Sundance, and Chance—present at the Sanctuary Ranch, Chance gave a little speech. He talked about the journey Esperanza had taken from that day of terror so long ago and how she had grown and changed into the blossoming, beautiful young woman they now beheld.

Tears of joy ran down Esperanza's pretty young face when Chance walked Rising Star out of the barn and ceremoniously handed the horse's lead rope to her. Chance also gave her a single eagle feather, a common but sacred American Indian gift.

Esperanza hugged everyone, even William Shakespeare, Butch, and Sundance, and she thanked them with all her heart for these gifts that left her in tears and nearly speechless.

All of the adults eventually left Esperanza alone with her new horse. They sat on the front porch of the ranch house where they could see the round pen and watch her groom her horse before saddling and riding. The beautiful girl on the stunning black horse was a sight to behold, they all agreed.

As they sat there admiring the young woman and her horse, who were beginning to get acquainted with each other, Alexis and Black Chief cornered Chance off to the side.

"Where did you get that eagle feather?" asked Alexis, an accusing tone in her voice.

"From an eagle," responded a smiling Chance.

"Please tell me you didn't steal that feather out of the evidence box from the Billy Big Bear and Jim Walking Horse investigation?" Alexis said.

Black Chief just smiled, shook his head at Chance, and quietly sighed. "Where else would he get it? It's illegal for anyone but an American Indian to possess an eagle feather. And an Indian can only have it for religious and ceremonial reasons."

Alexis continued to glare at Chance, waiting for him to answer her question.

Chance smiled a mischievous smile and answered, "What? I took one feather and I left one feather. Who's ever going to know? Besides, Billy Big Bear and Jim Walking Horse can't make good use of it anymore, so I thought it would be a nice little traditional and sacred gift for Esperanza. It will bring her luck and keep her safe through her travels in life." Chance grinned innocently.

"That's a potential $25,000 fine if she's caught with it," Alexis said. "You wouldn't put her at risk like that. What's the story?"

"Okay, you got me," Chance said. "Her parents told me that she's a registered member of the Gila River tribe through her maternal grandmother. So it's perfectly legal."

"You are really something, Chance Colt," said Alexis, doing her best to give him a stern look but unable to keep from grinning.

"Oh, that's what all the chicks say," said Chance.

"Well, at least you cleaned the dried blood off of it first," said Alexis.

With that, Black Chief let out a boisterous laugh, which made Alexis crack a smile that then quickly turned into quiet laughter, joining Black Chief's laughter with her own.

"All is good with the world, once again," Chance said, showing off his winning smile. "It's all good! Everything and everyone has returned back to complete and total harmony. Now let's just all sit back and enjoy the present moment, shall we?"

Chapter Eighteen

"Contemplation of my life decides the choice between advance and retreat."

~I Ching

Everything may have been harmonious on Chance's Sanctuary Ranch, but the world outside continued on its own chaotic downward spiral.

The frequent and unending violence on the Mexican border continued at a frantic pace. The deadly gun battles that seemed to be inbred into this part of the world had recently ratcheted up to an all-time high, generating a wave of violence in the seemingly never-ending infighting between the rival organized crime groups. They were continually vying for supremacy and control of the illegal drug trade in the state of Sonora, Mexico. Rival cartel factions struggled for control of the valuable territory for moving marijuana, heroin, cocaine, methamphetamines, and opium, along with illegal aliens, into the United States.

At the same time, moving in the opposite direction, guns and money were being transported from the United States into Mexico. AK-47s and AR-15 automatic rifles, shotguns, and their ammunition seem to be the weapons of choice. Both smuggling economies and industries seemed to support and finance each other in this wily, Wild West borderlands region.

The constant barrage of bullets rained down daily, like a hailstorm hitting on the tin roofs of the homes and communities of the small towns on either side of the border. In between these small towns there was nothing but miles and miles of open desert and mountains.

Official and unofficial accounts of the recent summer violence estimated the death toll of Sonoran state police officers, U.S. Border Patrol agents, drug cartel members, and innocent men, women, and children caught in the crossfire at forty to fifty people dead, along with dozens more injured. Many others were simply missing or unaccounted for. The death toll and violence were blamed on the constant battles and in-fighting between opposing cells of the two main Sinaloa, Mexico, drug cartels, known as Los Memos and Los Salazar.

This part of the world, it seemed, had been caught up in a constant and never-ending war of wills between cartels, countries, renegades, outlaws, cowboys, and Indians, since Spain invaded Mexico and the American Southwest hundreds of years ago.

In the midst of all of this constant chaos sat a peaceful former Marine, current lawman, and wannabe peaceful warrior trying to make some sense of it all. This man was Chance

Colt, a nineteenth century man trying to figure out how to survive in a twenty-first century world that had gone completely astray. He was a dinosaur facing the sad realization of eventual extinction, only he wasn't dead yet. He was a U.S. Marine who wouldn't retreat; a lawman who wouldn't retreat; and a man formed by chance and circumstance who wouldn't retreat. The option of retreat wasn't in his nature, and it never would be.

Chance had decided he was long overdue for some R&R and some alone time, so he took off for a three-day weekend, intending to camp by himself out under the stars on the other side of his hundred-acre ranch. He would do this every so often to get some peace and quiet and time to think and reflect on things, yet not be too far away from Sarah if she needed him.

There were several gravel service roads that he used to get to the southeastern corner of his ranch property in the old Blazer or on horseback. He liked to set up his two-man tent on a little escarpment of rock or a little butte or mesa that looked south down into the grassy valley below. On a clear day, he could see all the way to the mountains of northern Mexico, as the southern end of his property was only about twenty miles from the international border. Down here, in the Arizona borderlands country, the geography reminded Chance of East Africa, with its rolling hills and verdant valleys and green mountains.

He would camp alone for three days and two nights to rejuvenate his spirit and regain some inner peace that he constantly yearned for so often in his life. He had brought only two of his favorite books with him to read and think on: *No Death, No Fear,* written by the Vietnamese Buddhist Monk Thich Nhat Hanh, and *For Whom the Bell Tolls,* by Ernest Hemingway, arguably one of the best war novels ever written.

He also brought along his Colt .45 Model 1911 pistol and his trusty old Winchester Model 1894 30-30 long rifle for protection from the mountain lions, bobcats, and various other dangerous animals that occupied the region and also called this small piece of earth home.

He set up his tent and his camp next to the blue Blazer, parked high on a ridge, and sat quietly reading *No Death, No Fear* and enjoying the late afternoon sunshine. As dusk neared, he walked around the perimeter of his camp and collected firewood and kindling that he would use first to cook his dinner and later to keep warm, as the heat of the day gradually turned into the cool of the desert night.

He watched the sun sink over the Santa Rita Mountains to his west, as he cooked his dinner in a single frying pan over the smoldering fire of mesquite wood. He ate his rations in silence as his mind slipped back in time to his days in the Marine Corps. He thought of Operation Desert Storm and his early days in Saudi Arabia, Kuwait, and Iraq and later delved deep into the heart of darkness of his tour in Somalia, East Africa, where he killed more men on a so-called peace-keeping mission then he ever did in the war as a Marine scout sniper.

That particular piece of irony never ceased to amaze and confuse him, even now, after all of these years. He eventually, like always, chalked it up once again to the Three Constants of Life: Paradox, Humor, and Change. Some things in this world and in this life never would make sense to him, no matter how hard he thought on them.

As he watched the day turn into night, he concentrated with all of his senses of sight, sound, taste, touch, and smell and tuned into his wild surroundings. He saw many species of birds, a few lizards, and a couple of jack rabbits out scavenging for their evening meal; he listened to the songs of the birds, the slight sound of the wind rustling through the nearby trees, bushes and grasslands; breathed in and tasted the night-time desert and mountain air; touched the rapidly cooling earth with his hands; and smelled the clean creosote-scented air and mesquite-scented flames and smoke of his solitary campfire.

God, I love to be alone in the wild and in nature, he thought to himself. It was the best place for him to always find true and complete peace, both on the outside and on the inside; albeit only a temporary one, as he was always called back to his other world of work, duty, and responsibility. He often wished to himself that someday he and Sarah could ride their horses off into the wilderness, never to return to society again, and live out the rest of their days communing only with each other and with God and the nature that God had created for all beings to share and enjoy. It was a nice daydream to think about, anyway.

The sky was now a deep black hole, interspersed with a million shining stars. The stars reminded Chance briefly of Esperanza and her horse, Rising Star, and a smile crossed his lips. He lay down on his sleeping bag flat on his back to watch the celestial show in the night-time sky and fell sound asleep there next to the fire, under the wide-open sky, never making it into his tent.

He dreamt he was a bald eagle, soaring over an endless terrain of empty mountains and desert all alone, and he was at peace with himself and one with the entire universe. He slept deeply, peacefully and happily, soaring above the world on his strong, feathered wings, looking down in awe at God's green earth.

His temporarily blissful sleep was instantly shattered by thc familiar sound of gun shots, men's voices, and a truck engine roaring and racing in the valley below. Chance sat up quickly, zipped open his sleeping bag, and out of sheer habit grabbed for his boots and put them on. Even in the fog of sleep, he knew he wouldn't be going anywhere without them in the desert. As his brain and body slowly awoke into consciousness, he knew he was no longer an eagle and was now grounded back again on earth.

He was temporarily blinded by the glare of a pickup truck's spotlight and off-road lights, heading in his direction. He heard more cracks of sporadic gunfire and felt the bullets spray the ground around him and the smoldering remnants of his nearby campfire.

Chance jumped up and instinctively ran for his truck. He jumped in, started the old Blazer up, and flipped on his headlights and the police light-bar on the roof of his vehicle. With his lights on and his truck moving toward where the initial gunfire had originated from, he now clearly saw the Ford F-150 4X4 pickup truck approximately three hundred yards south of his position in the desert and moving toward him at a high rate of speed.

He flipped on the police siren and pulled his Colt .45 pistol from its holster on his left hip. He began to return gunfire at the on-rushing truck in front of him with his pistol snapping off a few rounds through his open driver's side window.

The F-150 suddenly stopped dead in its tracks about two hundred yards away, and both the driver's side door and the passenger door swung open and two men bailed out, quickly running off into the darkness of the black desert night. Chance then stopped his own truck, so he could pick up his Winchester rifle and quickly take aim at the two fleeing men. He managed to get off a few 150 grain power-point rounds in each man's general direction before losing sight of both men in the night.

With the F-150 now seemingly abandoned and the two shooters disappearing into the darkness, Chance stopped firing the big Winchester rifle, took a couple of deep breaths, and shook his head from side to side in a quick motion to wake himself up.

"Jesus Christ," he said aloud. His mouth was dry, and he gulped in a couple more deep breaths to provide his brain with some much-needed oxygen, so he could begin to comprehend what had just happened. He sat breathing heavily, his heart pounding from the adrenaline rush, as he reloaded seven more 30-30 shells into his rifle and placed a fresh, full clip into his .45 caliber pistol. He turned off his siren and light-bar and began shining his spotlight at the apparently abandoned F-150 pickup and around the general area, looking for the two armed men. They were nowhere in sight.

Chance waited about five minutes to think, catch his breath, and let the two gunmen continue to run south, hopefully. He began to think they were probably just two random Mexican drug smugglers who had accidently driven up to his campsite and tried to kill him just for being in their drug-running path in the middle of the night. He further assumed that once they knew he was an Arizona lawman, they quickly bailed and abandoned their truck and load, and were now high-tailing it back to the Mexican border and relative safety. That's what Chance wished for, at least.

He waited another few minutes to watch and listen before slowly driving his Blazer up to the F-150. He put the flashing lights of his light-bar back on to ensure if the two men were still within sight, they would realize without a doubt that he was an Arizona law enforcement officer.

He drove slowly in a full circle around the F-150 to make sure it was abandoned, and then he drove the Blazer in increasingly larger circles, searching for the two drug runners with his spotlight. After doing this for about fifteen minutes, he began to feel secure in the fact that the two men were gone, and he had the surrounding desert to himself. He drove back to the abandoned F-150 to search it and see what he would find. Whatever it was, it seemed to be important enough for them to want to kill him quickly.

Chance immediately saw that the F-150 truck bed was stuffed full of bails of marijuana, probably several hundred pounds worth. He parked his Blazer with his headlight high-beams lighting up the truck and surrounding vicinity, got out with his Winchester rifle held high and at the ready and searched the cab of the F-150. He found no weapons, drugs, or any other contraband in the cab of the truck, and he finally began to relax. His heart rate began to return to normal, and he began to laugh hysterically.

"What a score!" he said to no one in particular. "And in my own damn backyard." He laughed again.

He went back to his truck and radioed his county dispatcher and the Border Patrol with his location and discovery. He sat and watched in silence as a great-horned owl flew down noiselessly and perched in a nearby mesquite tree, glaring with beady, yellow eyes straight into Chance's soul.

"Great," Chance said aloud. According to Native American philosophy and traditions, the owl was considered a messenger from the dead. "Are you trying to tell me something? Otherwise, quit following me and let me be," Chance hollered in the owl's direction. The owl didn't move but just continued to blankly give Chance its death stare.

Approximately thirty minutes later one of his graveyard shift deputies and two green-and-white Border Patrol units arrived. Chance began his long story by explaining to his deputy and the Border Patrol agents why he happened by chance to be out there alone camping on his own land at 0400 hours in the morning. He described the actions of the driver of the Ford F-150 and the other person in the truck, both of who had fled; the shots fired; and the abandoned truck full of marijuana. The lawmen patiently listened to his colorful reenactment. The Border Patrol agents then called into their own radio dispatcher and supervisor to describe what had transpired, and they were immediately ordered by their command to secure the marijuana and call in a tow truck to impound the abandoned F-150.

Chance was curtly informed that the Border Patrol would be taking over the case from here, and the local sheriff and his deputy were to stand down. They were instantly relieved of their responsibility in the whole affair, which was fine with Chance. He just wanted to go back to sleep in his tent, and the feds could claim jurisdiction and authority over the whole mess. Chance just looked at his deputy and shrugged his shoulders, in what had become routine resignation when the feds claimed control and took credit for every drug find. Chance stepped aside with his bleary-eyed and tired-looking deputy, out of earshot of the feds.

"I'm going back to my tent and sleeping bag at my camp and hitting the sack," Chance informed his deputy, as the first signs of the new day began dawning on the eastern horizon. "Good night, deputy, and thanks for the back-up. Your shift is almost over, and you look like you need to go home and get some sleep yourself."

"Thanks, Sheriff," replied the deputy. "It's been a long night, and I am beat. Enjoy the rest of your camping weekend."

Chance walked back to his camp, grabbed his sleeping bag from next to the cold remains of his campfire, shook it out to ensure it was free of any poisonous desert critters, and went inside his tent. He proceeded to fall fast asleep within minutes of his tired, old body hitting the ground, but this time, he kept his boots on.

Chance was once again jarred awake from his deep sleep by the sound of a vehicle approaching and men's voices speaking in Spanish. He checked his watch: high noon. He poked his head out of his tent door and saw that the Border Patrol agents, the F-150, and all of the marijuana were gone, like they had never been there in the first place, as if last night's incident had all just been a bad dream. Such is daily life in the Arizona borderlands. However, now in their place was a sleek, black four-door Chevy Tahoe with shiny chrome wheels and black-tinted windows, which allowed no one to see who was inside.

Chance's heart sank at the sight of the truck, and he began to sweat—and not just from the noon-time heat. The two Hispanic men talking and walking around the area where the F-150 had earlier sat full of marijuana were most likely its original owners. The two men dressed in all black—black silk shirts unbuttoned halfway to their bellies, black dress pants, black cowboy hats, and black spit-shined cowboy boots—were angry and upset and looking for their abandoned cargo of illegal drugs. These men weren't the lowly drug mules Chance had earlier encountered in the dark of night. These two men were obviously professional businessmen and drug cartel kingpins looking for their booty—or for revenge, whichever came first.

They were armed with black AK-47 automatic rifles and walked in a small circle, speaking and swearing in Spanish about killing whoever was responsible for the hijacked shipment of their marijuana, along with killing the mother of the son of a bitch who had the *cojones* to steal from them and threaten their business and livelihood.

The two Mexican drug lords then glanced up at the Santa Cruz County Sheriff's Department vehicle parked on the ridge approximately three hundred yards away and glared at Chance's tent and campsite. Even at this distance, he could swear he saw the hatred and contempt burning in their dark, violent eyes.

Chance quickly pulled his head back into the interior of his little tent and hurriedly collected his .45 caliber pistol and Winchester rifle that were still fully loaded from last night. He contemplated making a mad dash from his tent to his truck. He was a sitting duck and soon to be a dead duck if he remained in the tent, so he would have to take his chances making a run for his truck.

As he exited his tent on a dead run armed with his pistol and rifle, he took one quick look out of the corner of his eye and saw the two armed Mexicans begin to run to their Chevy Tahoe. Chance swore at himself for not having the good sense to move his campsite after the excitement from last night. That was a dumb mistake and one he normally wouldn't have made, had he not been so tired.

Of course they interrogated the two hired mules who must have run all the way back to the border, while I stupidly went back to sleep in my tent, he thought to himself. *Now I'll have to face the consequences of that mistake—and what a deadly mistake it could be.*

But he was on his own land, damn it, and he was too proud and too stubborn to retreat.

There was only one alternative, and that was to do what he had been doing his whole adult life up until this very moment in time: fight! He instinctively knew that to fight or die were his only two options.

His mind was already made up as he made it safely to the driver's side of his old Blazer, opened the door, and dove in head first. By the time he had the Blazer started, his seat belt on, and the truck in gear, the Chevy Tahoe was coming at him fast with the two Mexican drug lords inside.

Chance managed to side swipe the Mexicans' truck as he began to play the old game of chicken with the other vehicle. As the two trucks briefly passed each other, they exchanged gunfire. Chance shot off a couple of rounds from his Colt .45 pistol out of his open window, as the Mexicans blasted a burst of automatic AK-47 fire into the steel side panels of Chance's Blazer.

Chance knew his old Blazer could never outrun the newer and faster Tahoe. The only chance he had was to play chicken with the Mexicans and try to take them out or shoot out their tires with some lucky shots from his pistol or rifle.

Both vehicles passed each other at high speed and drove in a large circle in the sand and dust to make another pass, like two steel medieval knights in shining armor entrenched in a jousting match to the death.

Chance could already smell the odor of leaking gasoline from his truck as he swung it around wide, creating a great cloud of dust. He drove straight back for another pass and shot at the speeding Tahoe. The initial spray of the AK-47 rounds must have punctured his gas tank or a fuel line, which was very bad news. He knew, however, if he could get close enough to the Tahoe, he had a chance of hitting the driver or a tire with his own small arms gunfire.

Chance aimed the old Blazer straight at the oncoming Tahoe, with his right hand on his steering wheel and his left hand gripping his Colt .45 pistol tightly, as he aimed his left arm outside the truck window and steadied his arm between the truck's door frame and his driver's side left-hand rearview mirror.

Chance swerved the Blazer to his right at the last possible moment, just avoiding hitting the Tahoe head-on. He slammed on his brakes to try to get one clear shot. He got his wish for only a split second and fired a round from his pistol at the Tahoe driver's head, as both vehicles briefly stopped in a cloud of sand and dust. His single .45 caliber round hit its mark, piercing the driver's head between his left temple and his left ear, splattering blood across the front windshield and interior of the vehicle, as his body slumped dead over the steering wheel.

That was a damn lucky shot, thought Chance. However, it didn't come without repercussions. The passenger of the Tahoe had fired another burst of automatic AK-47 rounds into the driver's side of Chance's open window, and he could feel the initial jolt and sting of some of the rounds hitting him.

Chance immediately knew he had been hit several times on his left side. His left hand, arm, and shoulder quickly went numb, and he saw his pistol fall from his left hand, permanently lost to the desert sand in a cloud of dust. He managed to hit his gas pedal with his right foot, pushing it all the way to the floorboard, as he spun away in the sand once more, away from the Tahoe. He drove about two hundred yards straight ahead, then made a wide turn of the steering wheel with his good right hand and arm and stopped the Blazer, waiting for the dust to settle, so he could locate his enemy once more. He watched the Tahoe passenger jump out of the passenger door of the truck, run around to the driver's side of the vehicle, and open the door. The man yanked his partner's dead body out of the truck and threw him off to the side, like a ragdoll, before jumping into the driver's seat, still carrying his AK-47 rifle. Chance saw him wipe away his dead partner's smeared blood from the windshield so he could see out of it again, and then he hit the gas, speeding the Tahoe toward Chance's Blazer.

Chance accelerated the Blazer in anticipation of another round of chicken, steering only with his good right hand. Since he couldn't pick up and shoot the Winchester rifle with one hand and steer the Blazer at the same time, he knew he was quickly running out of options to win the game and remain alive. In a last ditch effort, he knew he would not swerve this time at the last second. He knew he would aim for and try to hit the Tahoe head on, as he was now bleeding profusely from his numb left shoulder, arm, and hand.

The oncoming Tahoe slightly swerved to the right at the last moment, but it was too late to avoid the full impact of the two vehicles colliding nearly head-on, and the screeching, high-pitched sound of steel scraping steel drowned out the ringing random rounds of the AK-47 hitting Chance and his vehicle one last time.

The old Blazer careened to one side, sped down into a dry wash and rolled over twice, until it came to a dead stop lying on its roof in the middle of the dry riverbed in a final cloud of sand and dust. When the dust finally cleared, Chance realized he was still conscious and alive, but bleeding heavily from his numb left side, and he was hanging precariously upside down, trapped in his overturned Blazer by his seatbelt. He could not, no matter how much he painfully struggled, get the seatbelt to release from its latch on the seat that was now above him.

Chance was barely conscious and still bleeding heavily from his left shoulder, arm and hand, which were dangling lifeless and useless out at his side. He couldn't see the enemy Tahoe from his poor, trapped vantage point, so he had no idea if he had won the game of chicken or if his final assailant was dead or alive. His own life now hung precariously in the very real balance of his stuck seatbelt, with the smell of gasoline all around him and his truck.

Chance took a couple of deep breaths in an attempt to think clearly one last time before he figured he would pass out. *I thought seatbelts were supposed to save lives,* was all that came to his dazed and delirious mind.

"What a crock of shit that is," he said aloud. "Only God can save me now."

His ever-present guardian angel spoke up to give him some much-needed advice and direction. *You need to get the hell out of this truck, or you're gonna die the same way I did,* came the voice of the long-dead Sheriff George White.

"No shit, Sheriff!" Chance yelled back. "I'm not hanging here for my health. My seatbelt is stuck. I have a pocket knife in my right pants pocket that I'm trying to reach with my right arm and hand, but I'm not having much luck so far. If I can get to it, I can cut the seatbelt and try to crawl the hell out of here."

Hurry up! yelled the ghost of Sheriff White. *With the gas leaking, she's gonna blow.*

Chance reached out with his good right arm and hand to grasp the mic of his Motorola police radio. "Santa Cruz County from Unit 10," he bellowed into the mic.

"Go ahead, Unit 10," came Shirley's reassuring voice.

"Shirley, this is Chance. I have multiple gunshot wounds and I'm currently stuck hanging upside down in my vehicle in a dry wash at the southeast corner of my ranch property, just off the gravel access road. Gasoline is leaking out all over, and I need assistance before this truck blows up. Are there any available units in my vicinity?" he asked with an increasing urgency. "I need help, pronto, or I'm not gonna make it."

The radio crackled back with static. "Sheriff, this is Deputy Graves. I'm in your area near your ranch, and I'll be 10-23 to your location in five minutes."

"Well shit on a shingle," Chance said aloud. "Just my luck, I'm dying and I get Deputy Graves and his impeccable timing. I'm toast for sure now. I'm a dead duck. That damn owl was trying to give me a message. I should have heeded his warning. Soon Deputy Graves will be eating his lunch and his damn peanut butter and jelly sandwich all over the hood of his car next to my dead body."

He struggled again to reach the knife in his pocket. No luck. "Listen, Graves," Chance bellowed, "I don't have five minutes. You need to get here faster than that, or I'm dead. Do you understand me?"

"I'm on my way, Chief. Just hang on, and I'll be there."

"Why does he keep calling me chief?" Chance said aloud. "I'm dying here for God's sake, and he's still calling me chief. If I don't die, I'm gonna kill that son of a bitch!"

He keyed the mic again. "Listen up now Graves, do I look like a damn Indian chief to you? If you don't get here pronto, I'm gonna be a dead Indian chief—got it?"

Chance felt himself getting weaker, and he felt like he was about to lose consciousness at any second now from the large loss of blood.

"Graves, do you hear me?"

All Chance heard in return on the radio was just white noise; static.

"Graves?" Chance yelled again.

Static…

Chance looked up and could see that his brown felt cowboy hat had fallen off his head during the crash and was now lying face down on the back ceiling of his Blazer. *Shit,* he thought. He knew instinctively that his good luck had finally run out on him.

"Graves?" Chance called weakly into his radio mic one last time.

Static… Just continuous white noise and static.

And the once bright, sunny and harmonious world of Sheriff Chance Colt, U.S Marine, Arizona lawman, Zen master and peaceful warrior, slowly faded to a deep, dark black.

The End?

About the Author

Tom Hawks was born and raised in the Chicago, Illinois area. He holds a Bachelor of Science Degree in Criminal Justice Sciences from Illinois State University and is also a graduate of the Chicago Police Academy. He has worked as a Police Officer in the Chicago area and in private security, prior to entering the Casino Gaming industry, as a Casino Surveillance Director and Regulator.

Tom has lived and worked for over two decades in the casino surveillance and gaming regulatory fields for both commercially-owned Casino Hotel Resorts, as well as, Native American Tribes, in Las Vegas, Nevada, Arizona, Michigan, Illinois and Indiana.

He is an avid reader of both fiction and non-fiction in U.S. history, military arts and sciences, law enforcement, crime, criminology, leadership principles, Native American philosophy and Zen Buddhist philosophy. He considers himself to be a writer, philosopher, a student of Native American history, culture and philosophy and a student of Zen Buddhist history, culture and philosophy. He is also a modern-day cowboy, a poet, a peaceful warrior and a student of life. He believes that he was destined to be a writer, a philosopher, a Buddhist monk, a hermit, a Mountain Man or all of the above combined. He is a simple man with a simple plan, who proudly lives and will proudly die by The Code of the West.

Tom's life heroes and mentors include: his dad, his son, Mark Twain, Ernest Hemingway, the legendary Lakota Sioux warrior Crazy Horse, Henry David Thoreau, singer/song-writer/novelist and Calypso poet Jimmy Buffett and every dog and horse he has ever had the pleasure to share his life with.

Tom has lived in Arizona, Florida, Michigan, Nevada and Illinois. He currently resides in Sahuarita, Arizona, with his wife Lynn and his best friend, a black Labrador retriever named Cowboy. His philosophy and way of living his life can be summed up in one word: Simplify. He may be reached via his personal email address at tomahawktalk@yahoo.com. This is Tom's second published novel.

CPSIA information can be obtained
at www.ICGtesting.com
Printed in the USA
FSOW01n0448100916
24746FS

9 781621 833949